THE SHERIFF'S SECRET PAST

TINA RADCLIFFE

ISBN-13: 978-1-335-62164-1

Recycling programs for this product may not exist in your area.

The Sheriff's Secret Past

For questions and comments about the quality of this book, please contact us at CustomerService@Harlequin.com.

Love Inspired
22 Adelaide St. West, 41st Floor
Toronto, Ontario M5H 4E3, Canada
www.LoveInspired.com

HarperCollins Publishers
Macken House, 39/40 Mayor Street Upper,
Dublin 1, D01 C9W8, Ireland
www.HarperCollins.com

Printed in Lithuania

“Community is the best part of a small town.”

Emily continued, “And as sheriff, I suspect you’re in everyone’s business routinely.”

Chase reached for his coffee. “Maybe so, but I don’t go looking for trouble, and I keep my mouth closed.”

She shrugged and drizzled a copious amount of syrup from the little glass jar onto her pancakes. “I guess I’ll find out what I need to know when I complete an in-depth exposé on both candidates.”

Chase froze with his mug held midair. “What do you mean, in-depth exposé?”

“Your background, et cetera.”

Et cetera. Yeah, that was the part that concerned him. He’d come to Aspen Creek to escape the et cetera and never looked back. The last thing he needed was Emily Taylor digging into skeletons he’d long ago buried. Chase swallowed hard. He’d been a kid, barely seventeen, when it happened... He knew that, and yet his gut burned with shame.

Emily carefully wiped her mouth with her napkin. “Is that a problem?” She leaned forward with concern in her gaze. “Chase?”

“No. Not a problem. Why would it be?” He stared out the window, seeing nothing.

“You tell me.”

Tina Radcliffe has been dreaming and scribbling for years. Originally from Western New York, she left home for a tour of duty with the US Army Security Agency stationed in Augsburg, Germany, and ended up in Tulsa, Oklahoma. Her past careers include certified oncology RN, library cataloger and pharmacy clerk. She recently moved from Denver, Colorado, to the Phoenix, Arizona, area, where she writes heartwarming and fun inspirational romance.

Books by Tina Radcliffe

Love Inspired

Aspen Creek Cowboys

The Sheriff's Secret Past

Tumbleweed, Texas

The Pastor's Easter Prayer

Lazy M Ranch

The Baby Inheritance
The Cowboy Bargain
The Cowboy's Secret Past
The Cowboy's Forgotten Love

Hearts of Oklahoma

Finding the Road Home
Ready to Trust
His Holiday Prayer
The Cowgirl's Sacrifice

Big Heart Ranch

Claiming Her Cowboy
Falling for the Cowgirl
Christmas with the Cowboy
Her Last Chance Cowboy

Visit the Author Profile page at LoveInspired.com for more titles.

Trust in the Lord with all thine heart;
and lean not unto thine own understanding.
—*Proverbs* 3:5

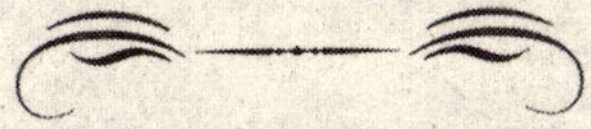

Dedicated to my dear Colorado friend and librarian, Sharon Medley, who believed in me, taught me the world according to Sharon, and will forever be "spot on." Here's to a life well lived. Brava, Sharon. Brava.

Chapter One

"I'm back!" Emily Taylor said the words to the empty office as she heaved a packing box onto the battered oak desk.

The new editor and publisher of the *Aspen Creek Journal* had returned to Aspen Creek, Colorado, just as she had vowed to one day. One summer during college, a mere two months, had changed the trajectory of her life. She'd fallen in love with journalism after her time in this small town.

It had taken twelve years to return, but she was here. *Thank You, Lord.*

Em took a deep breath and smiled. Though the old printing press had been retired years ago, the unmistakable scent of ink still lingered in the air, a testament to the history of the seventy-five-year-old weekly newspaper.

She inspected the office. It was just as she remembered from when she was here as an intern, the summer before her senior year. An erasable editorial calendar filled one white wall. Notes were scribbled on the board, along with doodles and various dates. A giant map of Aspen Creek and the surrounding towns had been haphazardly tacked behind the desk.

A sturdy oak coat-tree occupied one corner of the office, and in the other, a dented dark green metal file cabinet stood. On top of it sat a heartleaf philodendron in a brown pot. The ragged plant begged for attention, its scraggly tendrils reaching toward the sunlight of the only window in the office.

The office door was half frosted glass with an old, yellowing pull shade. A classic transom was overhead. Em crossed the room to look out the window. The stunning view right into the heart of the small Western town made her smile. The aspens on Main Street had begun to turn as night temperatures dipped with the promise of a new season. Their leaves fluttered in the early-September breeze. The merchant shops celebrated the end of summer with enticing displays in their windows. In the distance, she could see the jagged, snow-kissed caps of the San Juan Mountains to the west and a bright blue, cloudless sky above.

Her phone rang, and she fumbled in her purse for the device.

Douglas Baker. Her father.

Em hit the red end button. He was no doubt calling her once again in an attempt to lure her back into his world with the promise of a lucrative financial reward. She couldn't be bought. Somehow, he didn't get that. The high-profile criminal attorney who objectified his child and treated his multiple marriages like mergers was not welcome in her life at the moment. Though Em had taken her mother's maiden name to avoid her father's notoriety, he remained determined to bring her back into the Baker-dynasty fold.

The sound of boots tapping on the oak floors echoed through the reception area. Em turned around to see the retiring publisher and editor of the *Journal* in the doorway of the office.

Grace Stanton beamed. "Emily! What a wonderful Tuesday-morning surprise."

At seventysomething, Grace was every inch a powerhouse, small-town newspaper queen, even if her kingdom had fewer than twenty-five thousand citizens. She looked just as Em remembered: Grace's silver hair had been pulled back in an elegant twist, and she wore gray tweed slacks topped with a black cashmere sweater and silver-and-turquoise jewelry.

"Grace! How did you know I was here?"

"This is Aspen Creek, dear. And I assume that's your yellow Volkswagen Beetle at the curb. It's certainly in mint condition."

"Yes. It was my maternal grandmother's." Em couldn't help but smile. Driving the bright yellow vehicle brought back bittersweet memories of their last time together. She'd lost her mother at a young age, which made the recent passing of Gram even more difficult.

"Oh, Emily." Grace took Em's hand. "I am so sorry for your loss."

Em nodded. "Thank you. And thank you for the flowers."

"You're welcome." She paused, offering a tender smile. "What year is the car?"

"Nineteen sixty-three."

"How does she handle mountain roads?"

"Oh, that baby can do anything. She's fearless."

"Like you?" Grace raised a brow.

Em chuckled at the question. "I hope so."

"I've got a feeling you'll do fine in this town." Grace nodded with approval and glanced around. "So, what do you think of the place? We've made a few changes since you were in college." She chuckled. "Though not as many as I had hoped."

Em smiled. "It's as I remembered. If I close my eyes, I can see a bustling newspaper office straight out of a black-and-white movie."

Grace laughed. "We were never bustling, but this place does have history, as you probably recall." She waved a hand around the room toward the schoolhouse pendant light hanging on a metal chain and a stainless steel ceiling fan waiting for summer. "There's a conference room now, and I had the old printing press moved to the basement."

"You still have the press?"

"Yes, and it's all yours. Lock, stock and you know what. Who knows, you might find a buyer."

Em hesitated before plunging forward. "Um, Grace, do you mind if I ask you a personal question?"

"As long as my answer is off the record." Grace winked.

"Yes, of course." She chuckled. "Are you sure you want to sell the paper? Three generations of Stantons. That's a long time. I've spent a lifetime praying for roots like yours, and I can't imagine giving them up."

Grace smiled. "It's time. I'm not getting any younger, and I want the rest of my time here on earth to be with the only family I have left."

Em nodded. She could well relate to that, considering her father and a handful of stepbrothers she couldn't pick out of a lineup were her only relatives since her mother and grandmother were gone. Family was important. If you had one.

"I prayed and asked the Lord to bring along a buyer who would love the paper as my father and I have," Grace continued. "Someone who would understand that the paper is a ministry, God's work on earth." She swept a hand in front of Em. "Enter one Emily Taylor."

"I'm starting to wonder if I missed the Lord on this one," Em finally said.

"Why? I know the paper hasn't been performing as well as it should, but that's entirely my fault."

"Oh, no. I have faith in the weeklies. I've done my homework. I get that the newspaper industry has taken a hit and is struggling to find a place in the online world. However, the weekly is different. The weekly covers a slice of life that no one else can or will cover. And in a rural town like Aspen Creek, the *Journal* isn't going anywhere. I'm counting on that."

Grace's eyes lit up. "You do get it! I knew there was a reason we've kept in touch all these years." She took Em's hand. "If this paper is a calling, and I believe it is, then I know in my heart you are the one called. Take each day as it comes. Try to remember that your job is to pull the community together.

Let that thought be your yardstick when you have a decision to make. 'Will this decision unite Aspen Creek or tear it apart?' When in doubt, walk away, no matter how big or sensational the story."

"Thank you for that and for believing in me. I'm honored you think I'm capable of taking the reins." Em took a deep breath, grateful for the sage advice. Hopefully, she'd live up to Grace's faith in her.

"That summer you spent here, I knew you were special." Grace offered a musing smile. "I had several offers for the *Journal*. After all, it's not often a community paper is up for sale."

"Tell me about it. I've been looking across the country for an opportunity like this. When your email hit my inbox, I knew it was providence." Providence meant a chance to settle down after a childhood globe-trotting and a career that had her bouncing from job to job as the media industry evolved.

"You're the woman for this position, but make no mistake, you will have your work cut out for you. Circulation is down, and I'll be the first to admit it's more than likely because I'm a bit of a dinosaur. What this paper needs is someone like you to revitalize things. Not only are you energetic and full of great ideas, but you also have a fancy journalism degree as well."

Em smiled as she glanced at Grace's hand-tooled black-and-turquoise Western boots. "I couldn't hope to fill your shoes in a million years."

"Don't heap too many praises on me. On the contrary, you may want to strangle me very soon. Fortunately, I'll be gone by the time that happens. I'm leaving in the morning."

Em tensed, and a little voice inside begged for permission to scream. "Leaving?"

"My sister broke her hip. She's all alone in a big house outside of Boston. She's had a tough year. Multiple health issues, and now this. I must go."

Though she managed a sympathetic nod, Em's mind continued to wrestle with the fact that she would have to handle the paper alone.

It wasn't just the alone part that terrified her, but the "what if I mess this whole thing up" part. She certainly didn't want Grace to return only to discover that Em had single-handedly destroyed the newspaper that had been in the Stanton family for generations.

"Are you okay?" Grace asked.

Em opened her mouth to speak, but nothing came out. Her mind was stuck on another horrible image. Her bank account. She'd invested most of her life savings in the paper. Success was not optional.

"Breathe, honey," Grace said. "Harley will be here to assist you."

"Harley?"

"Harley Augustine."

The name rang a bell, a distant one. She'd been so preoccupied tying things up on the personal front that she couldn't recall half of what she and Grace had discussed.

"Your assistant," Grace prompted. "I brought her on board a few years ago."

"Yes. Yes. You said that she has worked part-time at the paper and part-time at the Aspen Creek Library."

Grace nodded. "Harley is a research gem. When it comes down to it, that gal picks up the balls I drop. You two will do fine."

"I hope so," Em murmured, though any confidence she felt up to this point had vanished.

"You have my phone number. If anything dire comes up, call me."

"Have a safe trip." Em offered the older woman a hug. As she stepped back, a movement out the window caught her attention. A law enforcement officer stood at the curb, eyeing her vehicle. A brown cowboy hat shielded his face, but the patch on his tan uniform sleeve identified him as a member of the Aspen Creek Sheriff's Department.

Realization hit Em. She gasped. "He can't do that."

"Who?" Grace asked.

"That deputy. He's ticketing my car." Em raced around the desk and nearly smacked into the door on her way out of the office.

"I'll check in with you once I reach Boston," Grace called.

"Thank you!" Racing outside, Em snatched the ticket from beneath her wiper blade and ran up to the police vehicle as the officer opened his door.

"Deputy!"

He turned, and in that moment, everything slowed down as Em realized she was face-to-face with Chase Everett.

Oh, my. Her heart began to beat a little faster, and her breath caught. The man was still as handsome as she remembered. His short hair, the color of milk chocolate, was visible beneath the cowboy hat that coordinated nicely with his tan uniform.

"Emily?" Chase blinked, obviously stunned. He shut the door of the vehicle with the Aspen Creek logo emblazoned on the side. "You're back."

"I am."

"When did you get to town?"

"Today."

"Today? No kidding. Well, on behalf of the good citizens of Aspen Creek, welcome back."

He stared at her for a long moment, as though trying to solve a puzzle. She met his gaze, recalling how easy it was to get lost in his eyes—hazel, splashed with hints of blue and green. Lost and not mind one bit.

Then her gaze landed on his badge, and Em stiffened. "Is this how you welcome everyone?" She waved the pink slip of paper in the air. "Seriously? A ticket? This is going to cost me forty bucks."

Chase plied the wrinkled ticket from her clenched fingers, smoothed the crumpled paper and looked it over. "That's yours? The yellow Volkswagen?"

She nodded.

"You were in a loading zone."

"I was unloading!"

"In front of the *Aspen Creek Journal*?" Chase pushed his hat back with a finger and narrowed his eyes. "Why would you be unloading in front of the newspaper office?"

"Because I'm the new editor and publisher, that's why."

His head jerked back. "So it's true. I heard that rumor six months ago and figured it was just that. A rumor."

"Why would you think that?"

"Because you didn't show up."

"It took me longer to get here than anticipated." She'd emptied her savings to purchase the paper, only to receive the news that her beloved maternal grandmother was dying. The long months of caring for her grandmother were followed by tying up the loose ends of Grams's modest estate after she passed.

"Twelve years, if my calculations are correct," Chase said. "Hard to believe a successful journalist would want to run a newspaper in a town that closes at 9:00 p.m. every night."

"Not any harder to believe than you being a deputy in a town that closes at 9:00 p.m."

"Sheriff. I'm the town's sheriff."

"The sheriff? Now I'm confused. I thought law enforcement in Aspen Creek was a short-term plan. Twelve years ago, you were headed to the Denver Police Department."

"Good memory." He eyed her as though surprised she recalled the detail.

That summer they'd shared a few conversations when they connected at community events, and Em had hung on his every word like the naïve college girl she was.

"I headed to Denver for the experience a big city police department could give me." He shrugged. "When Aspen Creek lost their sheriff, they asked me to consider returning. Turns out, I was ready for a slower pace." His phone pinged, and Chase glanced at his watch as if relieved. "I have to run. I've got a meeting in ten minutes. Could we chat another time?"

"How about a cup of coffee over at the Sunshine Diner? Say, three this afternoon?"

"I, um…" He pulled aviator sunglasses from his top pocket and slipped them on, as though putting a wall between them.

Em could see her reflection in the shiny lenses.

"I'm asking as the publisher and editor of the *Journal*. I'll be meeting with the mayor and the town council, too. This is business, Sheriff."

He hesitated before finally answering. "Sure. Three it is."

With a nod, Em marched back toward the *Journal* office. Then she stopped on the sidewalk. How did he know she was a successful journalist?

She started walking again, mulling the question and his attitude. Yes, okay. Perhaps Chase Everett did have a reason to be wary of her. Twelve years ago, she'd been rather tenacious. As a young, impressionable woman with no worldly experience, she'd fallen ridiculously hard and fast for the handsome deputy five years her senior. Chase had wisely kept her at arm's length, as though he too sensed the chemistry between them.

She shook her head as though shaking off the past. That was a long time ago, and much had happened in the years following her internship in Aspen Creek. Too much. Her father had lied to her about so many things that it had taken her years to find herself.

Chase was needlessly concerned. Emily Taylor was a different woman than the silly, flirtatious girl he'd met that summer. Discovering her father had bought her a fiancé had changed her outlook. She'd learned the price of misplaced trust and wouldn't make the mistake of being vulnerable again.

Em glanced at the shop windows as she walked back to the newspaper office and grinned, excitement bubbling up from deep inside. Oh, it was good to be back in Aspen Creek. The last time she was here, she and the Lord had gotten reacquainted. He had opened the doors for her return. She had high hopes for the same this time around, knowing Aspen Creek was a chance to make all her dreams come true.

Chase slapped his hat on his thigh in frustration as he strode down the sidewalk trying to wrap his mind around the meeting he'd just come from at the town hall.

Outmaneuvered. What stung was that it was by Vernon Rutherford, the wily mayor of Aspen Creek, who was aided and abetted by a few of his cronies on the town council. Whatever happened to sunshine laws? No doubt Vern would find a way to ensure it was all legal. It was a little suspicious, however, that he had waited until several key councilmen and women were in Denver for a weeklong conference.

Chase had only just found out that the mayor had held a meeting of the council last night. A meeting Chase hadn't been privy to. Vern had amended the Town of Aspen Creek's bylaws, tossing out a regulation prohibiting nepotism in employment. The mayor didn't plan to retire for another year, so he'd decided to change the law to accommodate his nephew as a ballot challenger for the sheriff position.

Yeah, and if that weren't annoying enough, they'd also added a write-in candidacy option for the November ballot. That was necessary, of course, since the younger Rutherford had missed the filing deadline.

Buster Rutherford, attorney at law.

While he tried to keep an open mind, Chase had to admit that when it came to most attorneys, his opinion was biased. Forgiveness was the key, but he wasn't there yet. No, the past still had a strong hold on him, even though he thought he'd moved on.

So the mayor's attorney nephew had his eye on Chase's job, and with the election nine weeks away, that meant only one thing to Chase. Politicking.

Which translated to people poking into his life. *Not going to happen.* He'd been cautious since he left home to erase every possible trail in an effort to keep his past from circling back to haunt him.

He didn't need that, especially now that he had his niece to consider. November wasn't just election time. November was one year since his sister, Phoebe, passed and marked the completion of the waiting period for kinship adoption. He would head to court to file a petition for the next phase of the process in adopting Phoebe's daughter, Sarah. The final step would be an appearance before the magistrate.

Good news on the horizon after a rough year. Seven-year-old Sarah had come to live with him last November after her mother died in a car accident. At the time, his mother, Hope, had been completing her cancer treatment, so he'd taken the decision about who would take care of Sarah away from her. Chase would adopt his niece. His mother had agreed, but only if she could come to Aspen Creek and help with the transition.

Chase was grateful because, as it turned out, besides being raw inside and out from his sister's passing, he didn't have a clue how to parent his niece.

The other issue causing his head to throb was campaigning. He wasn't a red-white-and-blue, baby-kissing, speeches-and-promises sort of guy. Never had to be. Fact was, the town had been so desperate for a sheriff four and a half years ago after the sudden passing of the former sheriff that the council had slapped the badge on him right after the interview. He'd transitioned from the Denver Police Department straight into his current position in Aspen Creek. Come fall, he'd run unopposed on the ballot.

Best-laid plans. He chuckled to himself.

Where did that leave him now? Chase shook his head. He liked his job and his new life in Aspen Creek. With a slower pace than Denver, the job allowed him to dispel the ghosts of the past. Except they hadn't gone away.

Right now, his past and his future were competing to keep him awake at night. The idea of running for office gave him indigestion on top of his irritation.

The sheriff of one of the smallest towns in Colorado would have to fight for the job he loved. Campaigning now until the November election wasn't exactly how he planned to spend his free time. He worked long and hard Monday through Friday so he could savor the weekend and devote more time to building a relationship with Sarah.

That said, he had his eye on the weather as well. Not many good fishing days left this time of year. Snow would blanket the town soon enough.

Shoving his hat back on, Chase headed toward the office and then stopped in the middle of the sidewalk. He shook his head and glanced at his watch.

It was well past three o'clock.

He groaned. If there was one thing he disliked more than surprises, it was being late.

Late to coffee with Emily Taylor was even worse. It was in his best interest to hold an upper hand with the woman.

Emily had only become more lovely with time, and the five-year age gap between them had become inconsequential. To make matters worse, Emily was smart. Smart enough to sniff out things he'd buried.

Chase had avoided her twelve years ago. It wouldn't be as simple now.

She was in Aspen Creek full-time. He was concerned. Absolutely concerned.

Thoughts elsewhere, Chase pushed open the door to the Sunshine Diner and stepped inside.

"Careful, Sheriff."

"What?" Chase blinked, realizing that he'd nearly run into the pint-size journalist. He stared into her wide brown eyes, his gaze traveling to her heart-shaped face framed by long, golden-brown hair, before lingering on her full pink lips. Wait a second. Was she leaving?

"I thought we had a… I thought…" Stumbling like a kid, Chase closed his mouth. Staring at her made him remember how scrambled his thoughts became when she was near.

"We did. But you're late, and I have an appointment," Emily said. "I don't have your phone number, and the movers just arrived with my furniture. I left a message with your assistant. Cora-Lee, right?" She waved a hand of dismissal and kept moving. "I've got to go."

Shoving her tote bag over her shoulder, Emily Taylor blew past him out the door.

Chase followed.

The woman kept walking, her pace increasing.

"Do you want some help?" he asked.

"No. But thank you." She tucked a lock of silky waves behind her ear, never breaking stride, in three-inch heels, no less.

He kept up—barely. "Are you living in town?" he asked, finally catching up enough to match her stride.

"Yes. Above the *Journal* until my condo sells. I imagine I'll be spending long hours at work for a while, so this arrangement will be satisfactory."

Farther down the street, a moving van's beep-beep-beep announced that it was backing up. The big truck lumbered backward until one of the fat, oversize rear tires edged over the curb.

Surely it would stop before it hit the parking meter.

It kept moving.

"Stop!" both Chase and Emily yelled at the same time.

The truck's bumper kissed the meter before it shuddered to a stop.

He cleared his throat. "Um… Do you want to reschedule coffee?" Chase didn't like failing to honor his commitments. Better to meet with Emily and find out her agenda now.

"Not necessary," she murmured. "You really don't want to chat or you would have shown up on time. Right?"

Ouch. Chase rubbed a hand along his jaw. "I apologize for not keeping our appointment."

Her hand shot up. "No worries, Sheriff."

"My name is Chase."

"I didn't want to presume." Emily offered a cordial nod. "Have a good day."

Without glancing back, she pulled open the side door of the building, the private entrance for the apartment above the storefront, and disappeared.

What was wrong with this picture? The last time she was in town, he practically had to hide from the woman. Now she'd dismissed him after accusing him of being unwelcoming.

Am I unwelcoming?

Guarded, maybe. And with good reason. But not unwelcoming.

He did an about-face to the moving truck.

The big back doors had groaned open.

"How can I help?" Chase asked a brawny guy wearing a long-sleeved black T-shirt who stood at the rear of the truck.

"You want to help?" The Ace Moving logo and the name Angelo were stitched on the front of his shirt.

"Sure. This is Aspen Creek. Rocky Mountain hospitality. If I lend a hand, you two will have time to head over to Sunshine Diner before you drive home."

"I like that plan. Let me check with the boss." Angelo jumped down and walked around to the driver to confer and returned, nodding. "Ace says knock yourself out."

"Thanks." Chase walked up the ramp to grab a cardboard box. Whoa. What did Emily have in here? Rocks? He rounded the building to the door where she had entered and looked up at the dark, narrow stairwell and endless steps that led to the second floor, wondering what he was doing. He ought to be running in the opposite direction of a journalist. They were in the same category as lawyers when it came to his past. Yet, he couldn't help the gut desire to prove he wasn't as inhospitable as she seemed to think.

"Where do you want this?" he asked when his boot hit the apartment's threshold.

"Excuse me?" Emily appeared from another room with a frown on her face. She'd ditched her skirt and heels for jeans and a sweatshirt and still managed to look like she'd stepped off the pages of a magazine. "What are you doing?"

"Being neighborly. The sooner I get your boxes up here, the sooner we can have coffee."

"Sheriff—"

He frowned.

"*Chase.* My window for coffee has closed. I have to get unpacked tonight. My first edition of the *Aspen Creek Journal* hits newsstands in one week. I have a full agenda."

"Not a problem. I'm still here to help." He paused. "And for the record, I pulled your ticket."

"Thank you." She rewarded him with a dazzling smile that nearly made him stumble. He glanced away, hoping she didn't notice, as the movers edged past him with a small kitchen table and chairs.

"So you're really here to stay."

"Why is that so hard to believe?"

"Except for tourists, most folks are counting the days to leave Aspen Creek and head to the city."

Em shrugged her shoulders. "I don't know what to tell you. This city girl is putting down roots."

Chase nodded, contemplating exactly what that meant as he started back down the steps for another load. He'd avoided entanglements all his life, preferring to date occasionally and end things before the relationship reached the bare-your-soul point. No use setting himself up for disappointment. The shame of his past remained in his closet, where it belonged.

Yeah, if there was one thing the past had taught him, it was that people were always willing to believe the worst. Like all the folks who'd believed he was guilty before he had his day in court.

Things were complicated now that there was Sarah and the upcoming family assessment by the courts to consider. He'd made a promise to his sister to take care of her daughter. A promise he intended to keep.

That meant that the best thing he could do was ignore his undeniable attraction to the *Journal*'s new editor. He'd managed to avoid her twelve years ago. Surely he could do it again. Right?

Chapter Two

Em rolled over and glanced around the room. Confused and shivering, she sat in a tangle of sheets and a blanket. The sun had risen, casting long morning shadows from the curtainless window into the room.

Startled, she tugged the corner of the blanket closer and grabbed her cell phone. Eight o'clock. She blinked, orienting herself. Aspen Creek, Colorado. Yes. Okay.

That didn't explain why it was so cold or who was banging.

The *Journal* office opened at nine. Em walked gingerly to the closet window, her toes curling with each step on the chilled hardwood floor.

Someone was outside. A female someone and her dog.

A glance down at her old, plaid pajamas had her hurrying into yesterday's clothes before racing down the short flight of steps and winding around the hall and through the *Journal* office. She unlatched both locks and yanked the heavy door open.

A petite young woman stood on the sidewalk, her shape hidden in an oversize army field jacket. Combat boots peeked out from beneath the hem of a long, patterned skirt. She had a perfectly oval face, turquoise eyes, scarlet Kewpie doll lips and waves of strawberry-blond hair. A pink Tupperware container was tucked under her arm.

The pup next to her cocked his head, a question on his face as he scrutinized the situation. Floppy ears framed a chocolate-

and-tan face. The furry body had patches of black, white and molasses.

"Hi, I'm Harley," the woman said.

"You're the librarian?" Em smiled, relieved that the cavalry had arrived.

"That's me."

"Come on in. I'm Emily Taylor." She stepped back as Harley stepped inside, while the dog sat quietly, waiting for permission.

"Don't you want your dog to come in, too?" Em asked.

"That's not my dog. He followed me here."

Em leaned down and inspected the animal. "No collar. Have you seen him around town?"

"No, although strays aren't uncommon around here. Occasionally city people drive through town and drop off animals."

"No. No. No." Emily grimaced, her heart aching as she considered Harley's explanation. "Please, please tell me that's not true."

"Sadly, it's very true. We're the country folks. They figure their unwanted pets are better off here. Too bad they don't consider that we have mountain lions here in the country."

Em fought the urge to put her fingers in her ears and yell, "La la la la."

Both Em and Harley stared down at the pup. He was obviously a mixed breed and one hundred percent adorable.

"Come on in, baby," Em finally said, opening the door even wider. "You'll be safe here."

The dog trotted past her, sniffed and began assessing the place, his little tail wagging as he went.

"You're keeping him?" Harley asked.

"I've at least got to let the vet check him out and then ask around to see if anyone is missing a dog."

"Then what?"

"I'm a one-step-at-a-time gal. I try to turn things over to the Lord." She smiled. "Not that I'm always successful."

"'The Lord is my helper, and I will not fear.' Hebrews 13:6." Harley nodded as she finished reciting.

Em stared at the librarian. "You know that right off the top of your head?"

"My father is the pastor of one of the Aspen Creek churches. Sort of another day for a PK."

"PK?"

"Preacher's kid."

"I see," Em answered, eyeing the librarian again. Clearly, there were many layers to her new friend.

"By the way," Harley said. "Good strategy. The day-by-day thing, especially the God part. You'll need some divine assistance for this job. That's for sure."

"What do you mean?" Em stared at Harley. The librarian's words echoed Grace's concern.

"The paper can be… Let me phrase this kindly." She pursed her lips. "The paper can be challenging."

"Challenging I can handle," Em returned. "My life has been nothing short of challenging of late."

"I guess that's good," Harley said. She glanced around. "So, you're living upstairs?"

"For the moment."

"Well then, welcome to Aspen Creek." Harley handed Em the Tupperware container. "Salted caramel brownies. They're my specialty."

Em couldn't help but grin as she accepted the gift. "Thank you! I can see we're going to be friends."

Harley's smile widened. "That was my plan."

"I have to ask, though. It's only eight. Why are you here so early?"

"I like to have things ready when Grace arrives." She moved toward the thermostat on the wall outside Em's office.

"Ready?"

"Turn on the furnace, make coffee."

"That explains why it feels like it's about forty degrees in here."

Harley glanced at the thermostat. "Spot-on. Forty degrees outside. Only about fifty in here."

"Fifty?"

Harley nodded and pulled fingerless black mittens from her pocket. "It's that time of year."

Em shivered and tucked her hands into the cuffs of her sweater. "I vote to turn on the furnace and leave it on. Especially since I'm living upstairs. Bare feet on a cold floor are a rude wake-up call."

"We can do that, though I have to warn you. The Beast is pretty old. That's why Grace waits as long as possible to turn it on."

"The Beast?"

"Yes. That's what she calls the furnace." Harley nodded toward a door. "Have you been down there?"

"No. The inspector did the dirty work for me when I bought the place." She hesitated. "I couldn't make the trip to Colorado at the time."

"You bought the place sight unseen?"

"More like hardly seen. I was here in college. Grace is a friend of one of my professors. He got me an internship here for the summer twelve years ago."

Harley's face registered confusion. "You really bought the paper without coming back to check things out?"

"Do you know how often a weekly paper in this part of the country is up for sale?" Em asked.

"Never?"

"Correct. I'm a journalist. This has been my dream for years. The paper was for sale at a reasonable price for this market. I've been praying for the Lord to lead me to the future He has for me. A future where I could stop traveling, settle down and establish roots." She lifted a hand in gesture. "If the Lord led me here, then I suppose it's up to Him to help me figure out how to succeed."

"I can get behind that plan." Harley lifted the plastic cover on the thermostat and adjusted the temperature dial. A loud heave rattled the room like a sleeping giant exhaling a breath. "There we go."

"That sounds like a beast, all right," Em said. "I know nothing about furnaces, but that can't be good. It sounds like there's some hesitation before igniting. The appraiser should have caught that."

"It doesn't make that noise every time. And it has a few more sounds in its repertoire."

"Of course it does. Now I'm sorry that I didn't buy the commercial property warranty." Em shook her head. "I'll see if I can get someone to come in and look at the Beast."

"Probably a good idea," Harley said. "You're good with me working mornings?"

"Of course. Don't you have a key?"

"I do. You locked the dead bolt."

"Oh, sorry. The doorknob seemed a bit sketchy. It wobbles. I'll get you a key to the dead bolt." Em ran a hand through her hair. "I'm going upstairs to my ice cave to get cleaned up. Are you okay with the dog here with you for a bit?"

"Sure. We'll be fine." Harley waved a hand. "I'll get him some water and put on the coffee." She paused, alarm on her face. "You do drink coffee, don't you?"

"Absolutely."

"Oh, I'm so glad." Harley beamed at the response.

Em hit the stairs. The apartment was wall-to-wall stacked boxes. After a quick washup, she wove her way to the closet where she'd stashed a suitcase and pulled out clean clothes.

Hesitating at the closet, she grabbed her coat and purse.

The aroma of coffee whispered sweet promises as Em started back down the steps. "What time does that grocery store on

Creek Street open?" she asked when she entered the newspaper office again.

"Not until nine." Harley handed Em a chipped mug full of coffee.

"Mmm, thanks. Have you had breakfast yet?"

"Oatmeal on a hot plate. Doesn't get any better than that."

"I had almond croissants from the bakery yesterday, so I'll have to argue that point."

"I concede immediately," Harley said. "If only I had time for another part-time job. Imagine working among those glass cases of pastries every day. Only one thing is better than the smell of fresh-baked goods."

"Is there anything better?"

"Yes. The aroma of a book."

"Says the librarian." Em sipped the hot coffee and nodded. "So why do you work at the *Journal*?"

"I like being desperately needed." She smiled. "In truth, I only have part-time hours at the library. I'm low on the totem pole."

"Do you live close by?"

"There's a restored Victorian around the block—Petal's Boardinghouse. You can't miss it. Pink and pinker. It's all one-room apartments. Short on space and overflowing with charm."

"Shared facilities?"

"Yes. Petal only rents to women. We share the living room and kitchen as well."

"If the furnace ends up a bust, I might have to check it out." She took a long drink of coffee and glanced around. "Where is the coffeemaker?"

"Down the hall. Our mini kitchen has a sink and a small fridge."

"Microwave?"

"We used to have a microwave, but it died."

Em made a mental note to pick up another. "Tell me a little about your schedule."

Harley grabbed a tote bag from a table near the entrance. She pulled out a laptop. "I'm here Monday through Friday, early a.m. until noon. I handle a few of the regular columns, like notices and obituaries. I also update the web version of the paper on Tuesdays. Today, I'm working on the layout. I'll send everything to Monte Vista early on Friday and the paper will come out on early Tuesday."

"Two-day lead time?"

"We're a small publication."

"Do they deliver it to us?"

"They're willing. The only catch is the price tag. Generally, Moss brings them to the office before he goes to work, unless the weather is tricky."

"Moss? His name is Moss? I thought Grace said his name was Ross."

Harley giggled. "No. It's Moss. Moss Boutilier. He works at the post office full-time and part-time at the paper."

"I see." She nodded, thinking. "Remind me about subscriptions."

"We have a delivery fella for the local subscriptions. The rest are labeled and delivered to the post office later in the day. I distribute the consignment copies to the merchants in town."

"I'm guessing that makes for a very long day."

"We all pitch in, but we couldn't do it without Moss. On Tuesdays he heads to Monte Vista before the sun rises."

"Why is he called Moss?" Em took a long swig of her coffee and stared at Harley with concern.

Harley cocked her head, giving the question some thought. "Got me. All I know is Moss has taken over coverage of high school sports, the crime beat, and he's also our photojournalist. He uses that small office next to the supply room when he's here."

"Is he ever in the office?"

"Usually late afternoons, unless he's traveling to a high school sports event."

"Can you contact him and ask what day works for a staff meeting?"

"Sure. You should know that we're short on features for next week's paper."

"Short on features for an edition that goes to press in less than two days?"

"Yes. I'm sorry."

"Is this normal?" Em asked.

"It has been lately. Grace has been so preoccupied with her sister and the move…" Harley gestured with a hand and grimaced. "We've been punting for weeks."

"Then I guess you and I will have to find news." Em walked to the kitchen. She placed her empty mug beside the coffeemaker and stepped across the hall to a small space no bigger than a closet. "Supply room?" Em asked as she assessed the nearly empty shelves.

Harley nodded.

"Looks like my work is cut out for me," Emily said. She returned to the reception area. "I'm going to the diner for breakfast. I'll see what I can dig up."

"Great. Oh, and Emily. You have to write an editorial."

Em froze. "An editorial." Somewhere in the recesses of her mind, she recalled that bit of information. "What do you suggest I write about?"

"This is the transition issue. Maybe a tribute to Grace?"

"That's a wonderful idea." Em pulled a business card from her purse. "Here's my email and phone number. Would you please send me a list of what you're already covering in this edition so I don't spin my wheels?"

"Got it."

"Thank you." Em frowned as she assessed the newspaper office once again. "Why is your desk so close to the front door? Isn't being in the middle of everything distracting?"

"We don't have a receptionist, and Grace likes me here to greet visitors," Harley said.

"Do we get a lot of visitors?"

Harley shook her head. "Sometimes business owners stop by to haggle over advertising rates."

"Hmm," Em murmured. She stepped into the conference room, to the left of the reception area. It boasted a gleaming oval conference table and chairs, a matching bookcase, and a file cabinet. An entire wall held a dry-erase board, while the opposing wall held black-and-white historical photos of the *Aspen Creek Journal* office through the years, matted in tones of sepia, with simple black frames. The room looked out on the town through storefront glass windows.

"How often is this space used?" Em asked.

"Only for staff meetings." Harley glanced into the empty room.

"This is now my office. You can take Grace's office." Em looked toward the front door. "I can see anyone who comes in from the conference room. I need to be the one to greet people and get to know the locals, don't you think?"

"Yes—" Harley gasped "—but are you sure? That's been the office of the editor in chief since the paper started."

"Now it's the office of the managing editor. Congratulations. You've been promoted."

Harley's eyes rounded. "Oh, my goodness. Thank you, Emily."

Em smiled. "Don't thank me. Promotions usually mean a raise and more work. All I have at the moment is more work."

"I'm up for it." Harley said with a grin. "Especially since I now have the window that faces the firehouse."

"I assume that's a good thing?"

"Oh, yes." Harley nodded and stared out the window, a swoony smile on her face.

Em smiled as she pulled on her coat. "What can I bring you back?"

"I'm fine."

"I insist."

"Well—" The redhead raised a brow. "I do have a penchant for carrot cake muffins from the diner."

"I'll bring them back after I find news." Em grabbed her purse and coat.

"What about the dog?" Harley asked.

"The dog." Em stared into the woeful eyes of the pup who sat in the corner. "Is there an animal shelter in town?" She pulled out her phone and snapped a photo of the dog.

"No, but there's a vet."

"Would you please call and schedule an appointment?" She exhaled. "I guess I better bring our sweet mutt back something to eat as well."

"Um, Emily? Where exactly are you going to find stories?" Harley asked.

"I don't know, but Grace said the paper should unite the community. All I have to do is come up with a few brilliant leads." She sighed. "Prayers are much welcome."

Chase leaned forward in his office chair and flipped the pages on his calendar. "What do you think about Friday and Saturday? Forecast says we have at least a week or two of pleasant weather. After that, who knows." He looked up at his friend, rancher Dylan Harris, seated in front of him.

Dylan shifted in his seat and stared at the floor. "I can't go."

"What? Why not? We haven't had a fishing weekend since spring." He needed the break more than ever. The constant self-doubts about whether he was qualified to be a father to Sarah, learning he had only weeks to create a political campaign, along with Emily Taylor's appearance, had him unable to sleep at night.

"I didn't think it was going to be this weekend. We've got our Fall Foliage event at the guest ranch. I can't take off."

"Your guests need help checking out the aspens turning color?"

"If only that was all it involved. We've got trail rides and picnics, along with a jamboree on Saturday evening."

"Sorry about that." Chase fiddled with the stack of papers on his desk. "I don't suppose your cousin is in town?"

"Matt? No. He's on the circuit clear through the holidays."

Chase shook his head.

"You know I'd be at the lake if I could."

"No worries, I'll catch a few trout in your honor."

"Who are you kidding? You won't give me two thoughts once you're leaning back with your line bobbing in the water and the sun lulling you to sleep." Dylan laughed.

"You're probably right," Chase said.

"So tell me about this campaign-for-your-job situation. More importantly, what's this news I'm hearing about Grace retiring and a new boss at the *Journal*?"

Chase shrugged. "Not much to tell."

"Heard she was crushing on you last time she was in town."

"That was twelve years ago. Who's feeding you this stuff?" Chase asked, though he knew the answer. The downside of a small town was how fast news traveled. He had long suspected that the CEO of the town's gossip mill was his office admin and part-time dispatcher, Cora-Lee Flanagan.

"To tell you the truth, I'm not sure. Overheard it in the diner."

"Whoever your source is, they're wrong." Chase cleared his throat. "As for the election, turns out I'm no longer running unopposed."

Dylan leaned closer in his chair. "Who's your opponent?"

"Buster Rutherford."

"What?" He shook his head, grimacing. "Buster is an ambulance chaser. The man isn't a serious contender."

Chase shrugged. "It is what it is. I'm going to need help strategizing." Even as he said the words, he tasted annoyance.

"Why not Cora-Lee? She'd make a great campaign manager."

"Cora-Lee Flanagan?"

"You know another Cora-Lee?" Dylan gave a belly laugh. "Chase, you've been battling with the woman for four years. It's a given that you're a saint. However, it seems apparent that this is the reason that the good Lord put her in your path. For this day."

Chase stared at the closed door that separated him from his admin, the widow of the former sheriff. Could he trust Cora-Lee with his campaign? The steps he took in the next weeks were more important than simply an election. He had Sarah's adoption to consider. It wouldn't bode well to go into the interview with the judge uncertain of his future.

"You think?" Chase finally asked.

"Yeah, I do," Dylan replied. "Let her do the work. I know from experience that this is her area of specialty."

"What specialty is that?"

"Cora-Lee's specialty is running roughshod on other people's business." Dylan chuckled. "All you have to do is give her your parameters and open the chute."

Chase shook his head. "I'll think on it. Though I have to tell you, somehow giving the fox the keys to the chicken coop doesn't seem too bright."

"You're smarter than the fox," Dylan said. "Remember that." He glanced at his watch, picked up his hat and stood. "Whatever you decide, I'm on Team Everett. You've got a heart for Aspen Creek. You're supposed to be here."

Chase glanced at his watch and stood as well. "Thanks, I appreciate the support." He grabbed his own hat and walked around the desk. "I'm going to pick up Sarah since school is out today. I promised her a muffin at the diner. You're welcome to join us."

"Can't. I've got a load of feed to pick up before I head back to the ranch." Dylan paused and looked at Chase. "How are things going with Sarah? Coming up on a year since she and your mother moved to Aspen Creek."

"Despite meeting with a therapist, Sarah is still struggling." Chase grimaced. They all were. Though time had passed, the grief remained raw.

"I'll be praying," Dylan said.

"Appreciate that."

Chase pulled open his office door and jerked back with surprise when he nearly ran into Cora-Lee. She straightened quickly and did her very best to appear nonchalant. With a hand, she tucked her gray bob behind her ears.

"Do you need something?" Chase asked.

"No," the admin replied. "Doing my normal morning routine. Dusting the furniture."

Dylan appeared to be holding back a laugh as he put his hat on and headed out the door.

Chase could only frown, electing not to ask why she didn't have a dust rag if she was dusting. "I'm heading down to the diner, but I'd appreciate it if you could set aside some time later. We need to talk."

"Everything okay, Sheriff?" she asked, her gaze uneasy.

"As good as can be for a Wednesday."

Stepping outside, Chase paused to take a deep breath. He loved this town. Over time, it had provided a balm for him, and he prayed it would be the same for Sarah. So he'd bite the bullet and ask for Cora-Lee's help.

Eventually.

After picking up Sarah at his house and saying goodbye to his mother, who was off to run an errand, he parked the truck on Main Street.

"Are you hungry?" he asked his niece. Chase held out a hand and assisted her from the back seat of the truck.

"Yes," she said softly.

Always polite, yet rarely speaking unless directly questioned, Sarah walked beside him. Her usual braids were missing today. Instead, her dark hair was loose, reminding him of his sister. Chase swallowed the pain that accompanied that realization. There were so many things about his niece that reminded him of Phoebe. Her laugh, for one. Except Sarah rarely laughed anymore.

As he and Sarah headed down the street, he spotted a familiar figure coming from the opposite direction, race-walking down the sidewalk, her head tucked into the collar of her coat. Emily. Chase's heart sped up as he looked around, searching for an escape route as she closed the distance between them.

There was none. His private and professional lives were about to collide, and there wasn't anything he could do about it.

They arrived at the diner entrance at the same time.

"Good morning, Emily," he said.

Her head popped up, and she shivered. "Good morning."

"Cold?" He asked the obvious, noting her red nose and rosy cheeks.

"Yes." She nodded, her eyes widening as she noticed Sarah at his side. Introductions were unavoidable. He could only pray things wouldn't get awkward.

"Emily, this is my niece, Sarah."

Sarah cocked her head and quietly assessed Emily.

"Sarah, this is Ms. Taylor. She is the boss of the town newspaper."

"The boss, huh?" Emily laughed, then smiled at Sarah. "It's so nice to meet you, Sarah. And you may call me Emily."

Chase's niece offered a shy nod, and he wasted no time quickly pulling open the door to the diner and gesturing for Emily to precede him into the warm shop.

For a moment, they stood in the small entry, scanning the interior as the savory scents of breakfast teased them.

Chase took a step toward the register and peeked into an alcove to the left. It seemed every booth and table were occupied.

"There's a booth in the corner," Emily said. "You two take it."

"No. You go ahead," Chase replied.

"We can all fit in the booth," a small voice said.

Chase blinked and looked down at his niece, stunned that she'd joined the conversation and unwilling to shut down her suggestion.

He looked at Sarah, then Emily. "She's right. We can all fit."

Emily hesitated, then nodded and offered a conciliatory smile. "Sure. Why not?"

Well, this was going to be interesting. He took Sarah's coat. Then, when Emily slipped off hers, he reached around to collect the plum-colored wool and placed it on a hook outside the booth.

"Thank you," Emily murmured. She slid into the booth across from him and Sarah and rubbed her hands together. "The *Journal* office is freezing. I had no idea it would be so cold at night this time of year. It's much warmer in Denver right now."

Chase nodded. "Wouldn't be surprised to see our first snowflakes soon as well." He smiled. "So you're here to thaw out?"

"Basically, yes." She tugged the sleeves of a nubby, multicolored sweater down farther and glanced around the room, excitement lighting up her brown eyes. "I'm also here to do some news gathering."

A mature white-haired gentleman passed their table, slowing for a moment to grin at Chase. "Hey, Sheriff, I heard you're no longer running unopposed. That true?" He narrowed his eyes in genial assessment. "Or is Vern full of hot air again?"

Chase shrugged. "Buster is running as a write-in candidate."

"Sounds like I'm right on both counts." Ralph winked.

"Now, Ralph, I didn't say that. You did," Chase responded.

The other man chuckled. “You know you have my vote.”

“Thanks.” Chase nodded toward Emily. “Ralph, have you met the new editor and publisher of the *Journal*? Emily Taylor?”

“No. Nice to meet you, ma'am. Welcome to town.”

“Thank you,” Emily replied.

“Ralph here is the local pharmacist.”

“Ah,” Emily said. “Good to know.”

“I'll leave you folks to your meal,” Ralph said with a smile.

Emily's eyes rounded when he left. “*An election!* That's news.”

“Not really.” Chase picked up a menu and studied it like he'd never seen it before, when, in fact, the Sunshine Diner's menu hadn't changed in years. Suddenly, inviting a journalist for breakfast didn't seem like such a wise move.

A young female server approached them and placed three glasses of water on the table.

“Hey there, Amy. Is the high school out today as well?” Chase asked.

“Sheriff Everett,” she huffed. “I'm not in high school anymore. I graduated last spring.”

“Oops. Sorry.” He looked up at her. “So, what are your plans?”

“I'm enrolled in cosmetology school.”

“Is that right?”

“Yes, sir. So be sure to leave me a big tip. I have a lot of expenses.” She winked at Emily, who smiled.

“I'll do that,” Chase said, turning over the menu.

Amy pulled an order pad and pen from her red-and-white-checkered apron. “Miss Sarah, what would you like?”

“A pumpkin muffin with a sausage patty, please,” Sarah said.

“Coffee?” Amy asked with a wink.

A slight smile lifted his niece's lips and she shook her head. “Milk, please.”

“The usual for you, Sheriff?” Amy asked.

"Yes, please. Oh, and Amy, this is Ms. Taylor, the new editor of the *Journal*."

"Pleased to meet you, ma'am."

"You, too, Amy," Emily said.

"So you came to Aspen Creek on purpose?" The young woman's brows knit together with apparent confusion.

"I did." Emily chuckled.

"Huh." Amy seemed to mull the concept for a moment. "What can I get for you, ma'am?"

"Black coffee and orange juice. Denver omelet, with a side of bacon." She looked up at Amy. "Could you substitute those dollar pancakes for the toast?"

"Surely," Amy said.

Emily tucked the menu away in its holder. "Oh, and may I please have two carrot cake muffins to go?"

"Absolutely." Amy nodded and turned from the table.

Chase's eyes rounded as his gaze met Emily's.

She shrugged. "I forgot to eat dinner. The muffins are for later."

He lifted his palms. "I didn't say a thing." Raised in an all-female household for much of his life, he knew better than to comment.

Amy returned with two black mugs dangling from her fingers and a carafe of coffee.

"Two coffees. Black. One milk coming up next," the young server said as she placed everything on the table and poured the coffee.

Emily wrapped her hands around the mug and watched the steam curl into the air. "So tell me about this election."

"Not much to tell." He glanced around, praying for a segue out of the topic of election news.

"Chase, either you share your information with me or I get the scoop elsewhere, and my source might not be as reliable. I'd much rather hear it from the candidate."

Resigned to the situation, Chase released a breath, slowly unfurled his napkin and placed it on his lap. "What do you want to know?"

"Who's the opposition?" She sipped her coffee.

"As I mentioned, Buster Rutherford is the write-in candidate. That much I did hear straight from the mayor."

"Why isn't he on the ballot?"

Chase picked up his coffee. "He missed the deadline to file."

"Then why is he an official candidate?"

"Just stating the facts, ma'am. You may want to speak to the mayor for the particulars." He shot a glance at his niece, then took a long swig of the dark brew, knowing he would need more than one cup to make it through this meal.

"Here we go," Amy said. She placed a white bag on the table and then slid their meals in front of them, along with Sarah's milk.

"Thank you so much," Emily said.

"Mind if I pray for the meal?" Chase asked Emily.

"Please do."

He took Sarah's hand and reached across the table for Emily's. Her slim fingers were warm from the coffee mug and fit nicely in his hand. Her eyes widened for a moment before she bowed her head.

"Lord," he began, "please bless this meal to our bodies and give us strength as we endeavor to do Your will today. Amen."

"Amen," Sarah whispered.

"Amen," Emily murmured, carefully disengaging her fingers.

"What are your plans for the day?" Chase asked as he reached for his fork. The best defense was always a good offense. If he kept Emily talking about herself and the paper, she wouldn't turn the conversation back on him.

"My to-do list is overflowing. I'd like to find a few good

stories for the paper, win a Pulitzer, buy a microwave and get the furnace fixed."

He smiled. "In any particular order?"

"Nope."

"Then try the hardware store first. They carry inexpensive microwaves. Save you a trip to the city."

"I'll do that, thank you." She picked up the saltshaker and sprinkled the seasoning on her eggs. "Any idea who I should contact about the furnace?"

"Bob Jones. In Paradise. Next town over. Best repairman in the three cities."

"Three cities meaning Paradise, Aspen Creek and Four Forks?"

"Yes, ma'am."

"Great. Oh, and that reminds me. Any reports of missing dogs? I found one. Well, technically, he found me."

Sarah perked up at the words and stopped eating. "A dog?" she asked quietly.

"That's right," Emily said with a smile.

"No reports. You could put up a flyer and check with the vet." Chase's attention remained on his niece's sudden interest as he replied to Emily.

"Where's the vet located?"

"Paws Veterinary Clinic is on the opposite end of town, on the right. Doc is getting ready to retire."

"What kind of dog?" Sarah asked.

"A giant fluffy black-and-white puppy." Emily pulled out her cell phone and swiped at the screen. "Here he is." She handed the phone to Sarah. "Do you like dogs?"

Sarah nodded as she studied the picture on Emily's phone. "He looks like Miss Tibbs."

Chase continued to follow the conversation in stunned surprise.

"Miss Tibbs. Is that your dog?" Emily asked.

Sarah gave a solemn shake of her head. "No. Miss Tibbs lived next door before I came here."

"Ah." Emily exchanged a look with Chase, as if sensing something was amiss. He tensed, expecting her to respond to the opening Sarah had laid down.

"How's your muffin?" Emily asked instead.

Sarah nodded and reached for her milk. "Good."

"My breakfast is good, too."

Chase relaxed. In five minutes, Emily had gotten more information from his niece than he had in the last year. Sarah liked dogs. Why didn't he know that?

"So, Sheriff," Emily said. "I'd love for you to write an op-ed piece for the *Journal*. What do you think?"

He chuckled. "No way. I have zero opinions, and I keep my nose out of everyone's business unless they break the law."

"Community is the best part of a small town, and as sheriff, I suspect you're in everyone's business routinely."

"Maybe so, but I don't go looking for trouble, and I keep my mouth closed." He reached for his coffee.

She shrugged and drizzled a copious amount of syrup from the little glass jar onto her pancakes. "I guess I'll find out what I need to know when I complete an in-depth exposé on both candidates."

Chase froze with his mug held midair. "What do you mean, in-depth exposé?"

"An in-depth look at the men running for office. Your background, et cetera."

Et cetera. Yeah, that was the part that concerned him. The last thing he needed was Emily Taylor digging into skeletons he'd long ago buried. Chase swallowed hard. He'd been a kid, barely seventeen, when he was acquitted. After enduring nearly two years of living in a powder keg situation with his stepfather, Chase had snapped in order to protect his mother and sister. The jury had agreed, and yet his gut still burned with shame.

Emily carefully wiped her lips with her napkin. "Is that a problem?"

He stared out the window, seeing nothing. Just like twenty years ago, he had a duty to protect his family. Chase vowed that Sarah would not be harmed by the shadow of his past.

"Chase?"

"No. Not a problem." He pushed his dish away. "Why would it be?"

"I don't know. You seemed…" Concern flashed across Emily's face. "Did I say something wrong?"

"Not a thing." He looked at Sarah, who'd finished off the last of her muffin. "Ready to go?"

His niece nodded, and he flagged down Amy with a hand. "Could you please box this up for me?"

"Sure, Sheriff." She scooped up the plate. "I'll meet you at the register."

Chase turned to Emily. "Breakfast is on me."

"No. I couldn't."

"Done deal." He mustered a smile he didn't feel as he grabbed Sarah's coat. "Have a good day, Ms. Editor."

Emily looked at him, frowning with confusion. "You as well." She offered Sarah a smile. "So nice to meet you, Sarah."

Sarah scooted from the bench, pausing to look at Emily. "Miss Tibbs had a red leash. Maybe you could get your dog a red leash."

A warm smile lit up Emily's face. "A red leash. Yes. That's a terrific idea. I'll be sure to get one. Thank you, Sarah."

Emily Taylor was a nice person. But she had no idea the power she had to stir up the past. *An exposé?* The word stalked him as he left the table. Someone uncovering his secrets was precisely what he did *not* need. And what about Sarah? What if an exposé became the reason for some social worker—or worse… a judge—to question his suitability as a parent? What then?

After ten months, his niece still hadn't come out of her protective shell of grief. Though this morning with Emily, she'd shown the first spark of curiosity that reminded him of the Sarah he used to visit in Denver.

His stomach churned as he stood at the counter. After leaving a hefty tip for Amy, he picked up the carryout box and held the door open for his niece.

His enthusiasm for talking to Cora-Lee about the campaign had waned. Yet, it had to be done. If he didn't win the election, he'd have to leave Aspen Creek and find another comparable salaried position. That meant uprooting Sarah again. Not an option.

So, yeah, after he dropped Sarah off with his mother, he'd speak to Cora-Lee, and make a few phone calls to Denver. It was time to check up on his past before his past caught up with him.

Chapter Three

Chase turned the corner and walked by the sheriff's office parking area. Cora-Lee, of course, had the spot closest to the door by virtue of seniority, or so she'd announced on his first day as sheriff four years ago.

Her space had her name in freshly painted black block letters. The spot had originally belonged to her late husband, Sheriff Tate Flanagan. Chase's space bore the faded name of a long-ago deputy on the cement curb.

Flanagan was a good guy—a fair sheriff. When Chase started his career in law enforcement twelve years ago as a deputy in Aspen Creek, he'd proved a fine mentor. In those days, Chase hadn't paid Cora-Lee much notice.

He did now. As the office admin, Cora-Lee was part of the package deal that came with the job. Usually the incoming sheriff hired his office staff. Cora-Lee's contract guaranteed her a position until she decided to retire or slipped her surly bonds.

He had resigned himself to neither ever occurring.

Though he and Cora-Lee had fallen into a companionable working relationship over the last few years, Chase struggled daily to keep her nose out of his personal business. Not that he had much of a personal life to start with. It was the principle of the thing.

The trouble was the late sheriff had managed the department with Cora-Lee as his adviser. She had a hard time with the fact that Chase didn't require her input on every decision. Granted, he'd be the first to admit that the woman sniffed out information better than a K-9. On occasion, that skill came in real handy.

He pulled open the door, stepped into the office and stared at the admin for a moment. As always, she sat ramrod straight, more focused than a drill sergeant and twice as foreboding. She wore a similar tan regulation uniform to the one he wore minus the badge.

"What was it you wanted to talk to me about, Sheriff?" she asked.

"I, uh..." Chase shoved his hands into his pockets and swallowed.

What was his hesitation? There were only nine weeks until the election. She'd get the campaign done, and as an added bonus, it would keep her occupied and out of his business. Dylan was right: Cora-Lee was the right person for the job if he wanted to win the election. And he had to.

He took a deep breath. This would prove to be one of the most challenging tasks of his life—asking the thorn in his side for help.

"Sheriff?"

"Yeah, sorry. Thinking." He approached her desk. "You may have heard that the mayor's nephew is also running for this office on a write-in ballot."

Fire sparked bright in her dark eyes. "Buster Rutherford is no more qualified to be sheriff than his uncle is to be mayor," she said evenly.

Chase nearly choked on that. "Mudslinging isn't what I had in mind."

"Had in mind for what?" She cocked her head and narrowed her eyes.

"My campaign. I'd like you to be my campaign manager."

In four years, he'd never seen Cora-Lee more surprised. Her eyes rounded, and her jaw became slack. Chase nearly laughed aloud. For the first time ever, he had gotten one over on Cora-Lee, and he'd dare to say that the woman was near speechless.

"I'm honored, Sheriff." A smile softened her angular face.

Savoring the moment, he turned toward his office. "Could you please hold my calls?"

"Yes, sir. I'll be sure not to let anyone disturb you."

He stood with his hand on the doorknob. "Thank you. Also, I'd like you to send flowers or a plant over to the *Aspen Creek Journal* from this office."

She raised her brows. "Anything in particular?"

He grimaced. "You're far more qualified than I am to make that decision. Something that says welcome. *Nothing more.*"

Still looking shell-shocked, Cora-Lee nodded. "Yes, sir. I'll get right on that."

Chase closed and locked the door. This was a wake-up call. He'd been going about this all wrong. His strategy had been defense, and for good reason, since his admin knew how to push his buttons. Often multiple buttons simultaneously.

Cora-Lee needed to be needed.

Who knew?

Chase turned on the fan in the corner. White noise to guarantee his conversation would not be overhead. Then he pulled out his cell phone. Another precaution. Chase never used the landline, which was connected to the phone at Cora-Lee's desk, for anything important.

He dialed the family attorney, Evan Blackwell, a close friend and, in many ways, his spiritual mentor. A man he couldn't help but think of like a father.

When the receptionist greeted him, he said, "Chase Everett, Sheriff's Department, Aspen Creek, Colorado. Is Evan available?"

"Yes, Sheriff. I'll connect you."

Barely a minute passed before a click on the line indicated his call had been transferred.

"Chase, how are you?" came Evan's voice.

"Good."

"You know you don't have to pull that sheriff card. She knows to put you through right away."

"It's the only time I get to pretend I'm important."

Evan chuckled. "What's up? You only call when you're worried about something."

"Is that right? If it is, I apologize."

"No problem. How's your mom doing? Is she still planning to move back to Denver once the adoption is finalized?"

"I'm not sure. She's taken early retirement from the college, but the cancer has made her determined to cross a few things off her bucket list before she makes any long-term decisions."

"Makes sense. And what about Sarah? Making any progress?"

"Slowly. She likes school, though she still doesn't verbalize much."

"On the other hand, you don't verbalize much, either." Evan paused. "How are you holding up?"

Chase sighed, knowing and appreciating that he could be honest with Evan. "I miss Phoebe. We all do."

"It's been a difficult year."

"Yeah. It has." Chase took a deep breath. "I'm calling because I want to run something by you."

"Shoot."

"Election time, and I find myself campaigning for my position here in Aspen Creek."

"Weren't you unopposed last time?"

"Yep. The only applicant for the position. This time, the mayor's nephew has his heart set on taking my place."

"I see. So you want to know how far inquiring minds have to dig to find anything."

"Exactly. In addition to being in the public eye for this campaign, there's also a brand-new, eager newspaper editor here in Aspen Creek." Chase toyed with the pens on his desk. "I admit, I'm worried."

"You haven't done anything wrong," Evan said firmly. "You were acquitted."

"I don't want anyone to even go there," Chase returned.

"I understand, but I'm sensing that you're ashamed, and I can give you half a dozen Bible verses telling you why you shouldn't be."

Chase closed his eyes for a moment as the familiar pain tried to choke him. "I killed my mother's husband."

"Shoving an angry man away from your mother before he struck her again saved her life. Probably your sister's as well. His death was an accident." Evan was silent a moment. "And Chase, it was twenty years ago. Nobody will find that story. It's buried. Besides, the courts never doubted that it was self-defense."

"That's not how the newspapers saw things. As I recall, my face was front and center in print for months, despite the fact that I was a juvenile. Being tried as an adult created a media circus."

"A good reporter would have taken the time to look at the whole story, not merely sensationalize the headlines to sell papers. Your family endured two years of abuse at the hands of your stepfather. It led to a moment that you're allowing to define your future. You're in law enforcement to prevent that sort of situation from happening to another family."

Chase couldn't deny the truth of his words.

Evan continued, "Besides, you changed your name. That's going to deter anyone digging around."

"Maybe," Chase murmured. Glancing down, he realized he had gripped the pen in his hand so tightly that it had bent to the point of snapping. He dropped the device on the desk and exhaled.

"No maybe about it. Remember that this is small-town politics. It's all about kissing babies and making speeches." He paused. "You passed the Denver Police background check without an issue, along with the background checks for your current position and for the adoption."

"Yeah, I've been fortunate to fly under the radar since I graduated from the academy. But like I said, there's a new editor at the helm of the *Aspen Creek Journal*, and my gut says I should be concerned."

"Is she a friend? If so, then maybe you should be up front with her. Tell her about Sarah."

"A friend? I'm not sure about that yet, and I can't see myself asking her to compromise her journalistic integrity and cover up a story."

"Then I suggest you start praying, because last time I checked, while you might be sheriff, God is still in charge."

"True enough." Chase exhaled. "Thanks for the advice. I appreciate it."

"If you need anything, let me know."

"I will. I will."

Chase disconnected, leaned back in the leather chair and folded his hands behind his head. Maybe he should consider pulling himself from the race. If it meant exposing the ugliness of the past again, he'd do it in a heartbeat to protect his mother and his niece.

One thing was certain: Until he decided how he would handle Emily examining his life with a microscope, he'd better keep her at arm's length once again.

When he finally stood and opened the door, he went straight for the coffeepot. He sniffed the brew to be sure it wasn't any of the flavored stuff Cora-Lee like to slip in on occasion.

"Sheriff?"

He turned to Cora-Lee, who held a clipboard and wore a solemn expression.

"I'm going to need some dates to work with for your fund-raising dinner," she said.

"Fund-raising?"

"Can't run a campaign without resources."

Chase ran a hand over his face. *So it begins.* He shook his head. "Fund-raising dinner. How's that work?"

"Your supporters buy a plate. You feed them, hire a small band or a deejay for entertainment and then give an inspiring speech." She shrugged. "That about sums it up."

"Make sure the food is tasty, because I can guarantee the speech won't be."

Cora-Lee fingered through the papers on her clipboard and jotted something down. "Yes, sir, I can do that. I'm going to guess this campaign will be easy-peasy."

"How do you figure that?"

"It will be in your favor that everyone likes you. Especially the single women."

She offered a knowing smile that had Chase moving back a step.

"Getting the local ranchers on your team won't take much, either. I'll speak to Nick Saunders. Then we can sit back and relax."

"Saunders?" Chase scrambled to figure out what the wealthy cattle baron had to do with his run for sheriff.

"He's the most influential man in the valley. As the Saunders Cattle Holdings votes, so votes the town."

Chase blinked. "You think Saunders is going to give me his support?"

"He's not a fan of the mayor."

That certainly put a spin on things. He met Cora-Lee's gaze. "I sure hope you're right about all this."

Cora-Lee tapped her pen on her clipboard. "I generally am. All you have to do is try not to irritate anyone between now and November."

"I'll do my best. However, you realize that the nature of the job means I'm going to make a percentage of the town unhappy."

"Yes. I'm simply suggesting you ease up on that. A few more friendly warnings and a few less forty-dollar tickets will keep everyone in Aspen Creek happy."

He shook his head, thinking of his encounter with Emily at the beginning of the week. "I'll see what I can do."

"Harley?" Em stood in the doorway of Harley's office. "Are the circulation stats current?" Em held her tablet in her hands and tapped her finger on the screen. "Including paid subscriptions and returns?"

Harley nodded.

Em pointed to a spreadsheet. "And these are our current advertisers?"

Once again, Harley nodded, this time cringing.

Her expression had Em nervous. "Grace admitted circ numbers were declining. This is more than that. I don't understand how things have deteriorated in six months since the audit I requested."

"I do the books, and I can tell you that it has been a slow decline."

"Do you always get a paycheck?"

"Oh, yes, though Grace hasn't drawn one in a while. She's been so preoccupied with her sister that she's often not here physically or mentally."

"Sure. I understand. I totally understand." *Been there and, sadly, done that this year.* She took some of the blame herself for not checking in with Grace and monitoring the financials on the paper. In her defense, taking care of her grandmother had encompassed her world for the last six months.

Em took a deep breath. "So basically, I'm not running the *Journal*. My mission is to *save* the *Journal*."

The room was silent for a moment, and then their eyes met.

"Yes, ma'am," Harley murmured. "I suppose that's correct."

"As long as we're both on the same page." Em offered a hollow chuckle at her pun.

Then she noticed Grace's half-dead plant on the file cabinet and released a sigh. "Could you put the philodendron in my office when you get a chance? While I'm saving the *Journal*, I may as well save that pitiful plant, too."

"Of course." The landline rang, and Harley grabbed it. "*Aspen Creek Journal.* Sure. Just a moment." She handed the receiver to Em. "For you."

Em moved the tablet to her other hand and took the phone.

"Ms. Taylor, this is Vesta over at the vet clinic. Your dog is ready."

"My dog?" She frowned and then remembered the dog that had showed up with Harley. "Oh, that stray I brought over this morning."

"Yes. The doctor gave him a complete physical. He's ready to go home." Vesta paused. "The dog. Not the doctor."

Em smiled. "No identification chip?"

"Nada. But he has been neutered."

"I see." Em paused. "Where's the nearest animal shelter?"

A painful gasp filled Em's ear, and she held the phone at a distance for a moment.

"You're not going to adopt this little baby?" Vesta asked.

"Me?" Growing up with her father, they'd owned purebred dogs handled by trainers and groomers. Beautiful animals, though she'd never been permitted to play with them. Sadly, there had never once been a stray mutt in the Baker home. As an adult, Emily hadn't lived in one place long enough to have a pet.

"I'd take him myself, except I already have three dogs and four cats," Vesta said. "My husband will have a conniption if I bring another one home. I might be able to sneak in a gerbil, but not another dog. He'd notice."

Em placed her palm over the phone and faced Harley. "I'm

guessing that having a dog at the boardinghouse is probably a no-no."

"You guessed right," Harley said.

She removed her hand. "Okay. I'll be right there." Em handed Harley the phone. "I'm a mother. I have to go pick up my baby."

"Congratulations. Big year for you. Publisher of the paper and motherhood."

"Yes. A very big year." Em slipped into her coat and headed out the door. "Unfortunately, not a very lucrative year so far."

She started down Main Street at a fast clip and then slowed to slip off her coat. The day had warmed, and the shop windows were too enticing to pass up. Time and again, she found herself pausing to gaze into the autumn displays in the windows.

At the corner, Em stopped. What was that lovely smell? She inhaled again. Bergamot? The main window of the corner shop had *House of Tea* stenciled on the window, and the front door was propped open to catch the breeze.

Em couldn't resist taking a step inside. She released a sound of delight as she glanced around. The interior was bathed in a soft glow from the twin set of cracked glass fixtures suspended overhead. Instead of traditional display cases, the tiny shop had antique cupboards and bureaus.

Em glanced at the ceiling and studied the tin ceiling tiles.

"I love those tiles, don't you? Adds character to the place."

Em whirled around to see a pretty brunette with a pixie cut, about her age, stocking the shelves. "It really does. What a lovely shop."

"Thank you."

Em stepped forward and offered her hand. "I'm sorry. I haven't introduced myself. Emily Taylor, editor in chief of the *Journal*."

"Ah, Emily Taylor. Grace had nothing but lovely things to say about you." She took the proffered hand. "I'm Sloane Flanagan."

"Flanagan. Like Cora-Lee Flanagan?" Em smiled, pleased at making the connection.

"Cora-Lee is my aunt."

Em nodded. "How do you feel about a feature story in the *Journal*?"

"That would be terrific advertising." Sloane's green eyes rounded as she smiled.

"I'll check the editorial calendar and we'll make that happen."

"I'd love that. Thank you," Sloane said with a clap of her hands.

"Terrific."

Delighted with her first merchant interaction, Em left the shop and continued down the street. She glanced at the architecture of several buildings, which had no doubt been erected when the town was founded over 125 years ago. There was a nostalgia piece waiting to be written. Nostalgia sold papers.

Unfortunately, it would be pretty much impossible to write up all these wonderful ideas before Friday's deadline for her first issue. She still had to do a final edit of her piece on Grace Stanton.

Pace yourself, Em. This is your forever home. You have plenty of time.

She grinned as she strode down the sidewalk, peeking in the shops shaded with identical black awnings. Gram would have loved Aspen Creek. Before she became ill, she and Gram had enjoyed prowling around small towns when Em visited her between assignments. The delight of uncovering the hidden charm of her new home eased the ache of her grandmother's passing.

Stopping at Paws Veterinary Clinic, she pulled open one of the double doors. It was quiet as a few dogs waited with their owners. The pooches dozing on the floor barely opened an eye to look at her when she came in. Their owners offered curious glances but said nothing. At the desk, a stout middle-aged woman hunched over the counter reading a newspaper. Engrossed, she snickered and then outright chuckled. Em leaned over to see what she was reading.

"Is that the *Paradise Gazette*?" Em asked. Why wasn't the woman reading the *Journal*?

The woman's head jerked up. She frowned at the interruption before quickly crumpling the pages closed and shoving the entire thing out of sight beneath the counter.

"Um, sorry. What was the question?"

"The paper. What was so interesting?" Em glanced at her name tag. So this was Vesta.

"The police reports. Hilarious. You can't make that stuff up."

"Police reports?"

"Yes. They put all the calls to the department in the *Paradise Gazette* each week."

"The *Journal* doesn't do that," Em returned.

"Maybe they ought to." Vesta slid the paper back onto the counter and folded a page back. "An emergency call came in at 2:00 a.m. on Tuesday. Mrs. Bernice Fogle called to report her apple pie had been stolen and requested extra patrol in the area." Vesta began to giggle. "Officers investigated and found the pie. No further action was taken."

"Where can I get a copy of the *Gazette*?" Em asked.

"The grocery carries all the local papers, and a few of the local businesses do as well. The *Gazette* is a weekly, like the *Journal*, except more fun. I subscribe. Can't miss a single issue." She paused to look Em up and down. "Excuse me. Who are you?"

"Emily Taylor, the new editor and publisher of the *Aspen Creek Journal*."

"Oh, Byron's momma. I'll get him for you." Vesta disappeared behind a closed door, leaving Em puzzled.

Did she say Byron*?* She turned and walked over to the literature rack.

Helpful Booklets, the sign read. Exactly what she needed. *The care and feeding of your dog. Vaccination questions answered. Health insurance for your pet.* She grabbed one of each of the twenty-four different booklets and shoved them in her purse.

"Here he is. Isn't he handsome?" Vesta grinned.

Em turned. The pup's multicolored fur had been fluffed and brushed, and someone had tied a navy-blue bandanna around his neck. Em's heart melted when he looked up at her, dark eyes round and hopeful.

"We took the liberty of giving Byron a bath today. Tolerated it like a champ. Didn't even fuss when the groomer blow-dried him."

"Byron?" Em asked.

"The doctor says he's a mix. Bernese mountain dog and Labrador retriever. A Labernese."

"Labernese." Em nodded. "And why Byron?"

"We can't call him Dog all day. I tried a few names. When I said Byron, he perked up."

"Okay. Byron works, and there's a literary reference in there." Em assessed her dog. "How old is he?"

"Doc says he's about nine months old. Do you want to wait to talk to the doc?" Vesta glanced at Em's naked ring finger, then leaned close. "By the way, we have a new doc joining us soon. Dr. Morris. He's single."

Em's eyes popped at the words. "Ah, good to know." She cleared her throat. "I'm fine, unless Byron has issues I need to know about."

"No, he's healthy as can be. Probably dropped off, is our guess. Got too big too fast for the owner. Adorable dog. This breed is kid-friendly, but he's going to be huge."

"How huge?"

"Eighty to one hundred pounds. Maybe bigger."

Em's eyes popped wide at the answer. "Not a lapdog."

"Does that sound like a lapdog?" Vesta asked, one hand on her ample hip.

"I suppose not." Em glanced at Byron. "What's the best thing to feed him?"

Vesta pointed to a prominent display of special veterinary food and animal supplies. "We highly recommend this brand—less filler. We have starter bags. Then you can go online and order regular deliveries." She moved over to the rack to grab a brochure. "Here's more information on Byron's dietary needs."

"Oh, I have that one," Em said, opening her purse.

Vesta glanced at the purse, chock-full of booklets, and her eyes rounded. "The library can give you a card if you're short on reading material."

"Good idea. Libraries have books on the care and feeding of dogs, too." She smiled. "If I'm keeping him, I want to do everything correctly."

"That's the attitude." Vesta plopped a hefty five-pound bag of dog food on the counter.

"That's a starter bag?"

"For this dog it is."

Em began mental budget calculations. "Anything else?"

"Doc gave him his initial vaccinations. We'll call when it's time for more."

Byron whined at the words.

"In the meantime, this card has our hours, and the groomer's as well."

"Thank you."

"Do you need any chew toys or maybe a doggie bed?"

"Can I buy that elsewhere?"

"Of course. But you'll have to take a drive for that."

She didn't have time to take a drive right now. Em looked from the display to Byron. "I'll take one chew toy and a doggie bed, please." Em paused, recalling the conversation with

Chase's niece this morning. "Oh, and I need a leash. Do you have a red one?"

"Sure do." Vesta rang up the amount and smiled as she rattled off the total. "I gave you the leash and collar at no charge since you're such a good customer."

"Thanks. Man's best friend isn't cheap." Em reached for her debit card, her stomach queasy.

"Yes, but this is the best investment you'll ever make. I promise you."

"Only if he can write feature articles," Em muttered. There would be no more muffins at the Sunshine Diner until the check for her last freelance assignment showed up or her condo in Denver sold. She might be eating kibble if her finances didn't look up soon.

She clicked the leash onto Byron's collar and wrapped the handle around her wrist. Then she grabbed the plastic bag carrying the fuzzy bed and the chew toy and wrapped her other arm around the bag of dry dog food.

"You want some help?" Vesta asked.

"No, thanks. I've got this." She led the energetic pup out of the vet's and onto the sidewalk. "Okay, pal, we're going to have to be economical for a while. That means you better chew slowly."

"What a sweet dog," a woman said as Em and Byron raced past.

"Thank you," Em called over her shoulder, while Byron started to trot like he had someplace to be. They moved down Main Street and right past the *Journal* office.

"Whoa. Stop." Byron did neither. Failing to recite the proper command, Em realized the only way she could stop the dog was to stop moving. She barely managed to back up and grasp the doorknob of the newspaper office and open it. Byron got the message and dragged her inside.

Em shoved the packages onto the reception table and collapsed into a chair, panting.

"Look at him!" Harley cried.

"He's been christened Byron by Vesta at the vet office."

"*Lord Byron.* I love that name. He's beautiful." Harley knelt beside the pup and rubbed his glossy fur while Em removed the leash.

"He ought to be beautiful. This dog cost more than a spa day." She picked fur off her sweater.

"Do you do spa days?" Harley asked, her eyes filled with awe.

"Not lately." She pulled the flannel dog bed out of the bag. "Would you mind getting his bed set up while I run to the grocery store for a copy of the *Paradise Gazette*?"

"The *Gazette*?"

"I want to check out the competition. Do you ever read the Paradise paper?"

"Sure, a few times. I mean, the library gets all the area weeklies."

"Brilliant. I'll get a library card while I'm at it." She paused. "Also, what can you tell me about Sheriff Everett?"

"Chase?" Harley glanced out the window and then back at Em. "Well, he's best friends with Dylan Harris, who runs the guest ranch outside town."

"That's all you know about the sheriff?"

"Sometimes he comes by the library for story hour with his niece, Sarah. She's about seven."

Em nodded. "He stays for story hour?"

"Uh-huh. He sits on the floor with her for the entire hour."

"Huh." Em tried to wrap her head around the stoic law enforcement officer sitting on the floor with a group of kids. Perhaps she'd underestimated Chase. Maybe he was one of those tough on the outside and soft on the inside guys. That was not without its appeal.

"I forgot to mention that I met Sarah this morning. She's very shy, isn't she?" Em continued.

"Maybe *somber* is a better word," Harley said. "It's a sad story. His sister was a single mother, and she passed last year. Chase's mom moved to Aspen Creek to help Chase with Sarah."

"Oh, my." Em sucked in a breath. A little girl without her momma. That hit too close to home. She'd lost her own mother at the same age. Except she didn't have an uncle to lean on. Only a father who wasn't comfortable with children and turned her care over to a nanny.

"So Chase is the child's guardian?"

Harley nodded her head. "That's what I hear from Dylan. Chase plans to adopt her." She inched nearer to the window as she spoke, a wistful smile lifting her lips.

"No ex-wife? Girlfriends?" Em knew it really wasn't any of her business, but a small part of her couldn't help but be curious now.

Harley shrugged, her focus on the street. "I don't think so."

The answer wasn't exactly conclusive. Em moved closer to the window, too. "What are you looking at?"

"Hmm?"

"I asked what you're looking at."

Harley sighed, her nose now nearly pressed against the glass. "Ryan Murphy."

Em glanced at the group of Aspen Creek volunteer firefighters in blue uniform pants and T-shirts, draining the hydrant a few doors down. "A rather fit bunch, aren't they? Which one of those nice gentlemen is Ryan?"

"The handsome one."

Em chuckled. "Could you be more specific?"

"The handsome guy with the unruly blond hair and dimples."

"Ah, the laughing one."

"Yes. That's Murph. Always laughing."

"Is he aware of your feelings?"

"My what?" Harley tore her gaze away and looked at Em, distress in her eyes.

"It's pretty obvious."

"Is it?" Harley bit her lip. "Oh, no. Murph is a good friend. That's all. We both grew up in Aspen Creek, and we've known each other since kindergarten. Ryan's family owns the hardware store and Ryan runs the place."

"That's great. You know, friendships provide a foundation for lasting relationships."

"What? No." Harley seemed startled at the question. She shook her head and ran her fingers through her curls, avoiding Em's gaze. "Murph will never think of me as anything other than a buddy. He calls me nearly every night to discuss his life."

"Hmm. Have you considered changing the way that he sees you?"

"I don't follow."

"It's often helpful to be less available. Right now, you're familiar. Like a favorite shirt. Comfortable. If you become a little more unavailable, I can guarantee he'll pay attention."

"Unavailable?" Her eyes rounded with confusion. "How would I do that?"

"Stop answering when he calls."

"What do you mean?" Harley's face reflected horror.

"I mean, stop answering." The solution seemed clear to Em.

Byron sat watching them, his gaze moving from one woman to the other.

"Not answer? I can't do that," Harley protested.

"Wait a minute," Em said, a surge of inspiration filling her. "This is it. This is the first letter for our advice column."

Byron offered an enthusiastic bark and raced in a circle, his tongue lolling with joy.

"We don't have an advice column."

"We do now." Em pulled her computer tablet from her bag. "We have just enough time to get this in my first issue."

"What?" Harley blinked, her jaw slack.

"Don't worry, I won't use your name. This will be our inaugural letter. Friends-to-more. That's a romance trope that most women can relate to."

"You're kidding, right?"

"No. I'm not." Em paused, thinking. "This will sell papers. We just have to find a catchy name for the column."

"I suppose it will," Harley murmured. She fiddled with the hem of her sweater.

Em looked at her. "What's wrong?"

"It's fine and dandy to give imaginary advice in a column, but this is my life. What will I say when Murphy calls?"

"Why do you call him Murphy if his name is Ryan?"

"Everyone calls him Murphy or Murph."

Em shook her head. "Not anymore. Call him Ryan. Be the woman who calls him by his given name."

"Does it matter?"

"Yes. You are not one of the guys." With one broken engagement under her belt, Em knew she was far from a relationship expert, but knew how the male ego worked, thanks to observing her father and her former fiancé. Their interest grew with a fervor when a woman showed disinterest. Which explained her father's three ex-wives.

"Oh?" Harley's face brightened. "Oh! I get it."

"Now, what are you going to do when he calls?"

"Not answer." She gave a quick nod, followed by a frown. "But I'll eventually run into him." Harley sighed. "He knows I work at the library until five."

"You'll have to find something to do after that."

"What?" she asked. "I usually go home."

"Aren't there other options?"

"They do have adult education classes at the high school in the evenings. There's a pottery class I've wanted to take." She chewed a nail. "I never have because I wanted to be home in case Murph called." Her gaze met Em's, and she cringed.

Em resisted the urge to point out the obvious.

Harley turned back to the window again. She shook her head slowly. "I'm like a giant Labrador retriever, following him around, rolling over for a belly rub and waiting for scraps of attention."

"I don't think it's quite that dire."

"Yes, it is. You're right. My Murphy-worshipping days are over." Harley pulled back her shoulders. She looked at Em. "What are you doing tonight?"

"Writing an editorial and our new advice column."

"I suppose I could take my little brother to the movies," Harley said. "He's always bugging me to."

"Great idea," Em said. "You know, I nearly forgot about the old movie theater across from the town square. Great example of Art Deco. There's a feature story for another day." She stepped into the reception area and grabbed her tote. "I've got to get going. My list of errands is a mile long."

"You've been busy all morning. Now what?"

"A stop at the hardware store for a spare key for the dead bolt and to buy a microwave. Then grocery shopping." Em typed a list on her tablet. "When you get a minute, can you compile a list of the merchants who carry the *Journal* for me?"

"Sure."

Em glanced at her watch. "I better get a move on," she said. "Time is money, and we don't have much of either. Getting these errands done will get me on track, which will go a long way toward me sleeping at night."

"I'm sorry, Emily. You've been handed a mess. I guess I just got so used to things being like this. Is there anything else I can do to help?"

"You could call Bob Jones in Paradise for me and schedule a time to check the furnace."

"Consider it done. What else?"

"Tell me the location of the nearest park. I'll need to start walking Byron in the morning and evening to burn off some of his energy."

Harley brightened, and she looked at the frisky pup playing with the chew toy he'd pulled from the shopping bag around the reception area. "Are you keeping him?"

"I'll put his picture in the paper and see if anyone steps up to claim him." She sighed. "After that, I'm not sure what I'm doing."

Harley nodded. "The park is two blocks over on Aspen Leaf, across from the elementary school. There's a dog park right behind the public park."

"Thank you." She scooped her keys from her pocket. "If I'm not back when you have to leave, would you check his food and water and lock up the office?"

"Of course. Anything else?"

"Pray. Lots of prayers would be appreciated. Pray we can save the *Journal*."

Chapter Four

The front door of the *Journal* office opened, and Em blinked, realizing she'd nodded off doing paperwork.

"Hello. Anyone here?"

"Yes. In the conference room."

Scrambling out of her chair, Em's gaze shot to the ancient conference room clock. Three o'clock on a Friday.

An attractive woman in her forties with wavy black hair that fell to her shoulders waited in the reception area, where Byron inspected her shoes. She held a brushed copper planter with embossed trim. It overflowed with assorted plants.

"Hi, there," she said. "You must be Emily Taylor."

Em stifled a yawn. "Yes. Yes, I am."

The woman offered a hand. "Lucy Reynolds from Lucinda's Florals and Home Decor."

"Nice to meet you." Em shook her hand and smiled. "You're down the street next to the bakery, right?"

"That's me." She offered the container to Em, who took it. "These are for you. The card is inside, and there's a care and feeding guide in the envelope as well." She smiled. "Oh, I nearly forgot." She fished in her jeans pocket and pulled out a piece of paper and handed it to Em. "This is from me. Forty percent off your first purchase of our home decor items. We're glad to have you here."

"Thank you so much." A rush of warmth filled Em at the gesture.

"My pleasure. Welcome to Aspen Creek. If there's anything I can do to help you settle in, let me know."

"I will. Thanks again."

"Nice dog," Lucy added. She gave Byron's head a rub, nodded to Em and was out the door.

Byron followed Em as she placed the planter in the middle of the conference room table and plucked out the card. "Look at this, Byron. It says, 'Welcome to Aspen Creek, from the Sheriff's Department.'"

What a lovely gesture from Chase. Perhaps a journalist of many words and a sheriff of few could find a middle ground. Em laughed at the thought.

Her glance went to the clock again. Time to call it a week. The transition issue of the paper had been put to bed, albeit a few hours later than expected. It featured a tribute to Grace Stanton along with a timeline of the history of the *Journal*. The issue also included an article on the upcoming sheriff election and a few other ballot line items for the town's voters, and it debuted the new advice column, christened *Dispatches from the Heart*. There was also a picture of Byron in there. Though Em wasn't eager to part with the pup, making sure he wasn't someone's missing pet was the right thing to do.

Tuesday, the first edition of the *Journal* with her name on the masthead would go out into the world. She couldn't wait for the community response.

She'd met with her team earlier in the day for a productive planning session. Moss Boutilier had turned out to be as insightful as he was quirky. How many mail carriers tucked a red silk cravat into their shirt pocket? With a shaved head and long limbs, the six-foot-five photojournalist towered over her and Harley. A creative soul, Moss would bring much to the team.

Two factors would determine the future of the paper: increasing the advertising dollars from the local merchants and creating content excitement. Em looked forward to changing things up at the *Journal* and grabbing the interest of the citizens of Aspen Creek. Harley and Moss could help her revitalize the content.

Hopefully, that would equal more sales, because there were bills to be paid, including the pending outcome on the repair of the Beast. Bob Jones had stopped by and promised to do his best to repair the furnace enough to limp along one more season.

If not, she feared replacing the furnace would mean she'd have to let go of staff until the paper was in the black again. And what if they didn't get in the black? Em shuddered. She'd only just arrived. She wasn't ready to leave Aspen Creek, especially as a failure. That would be exactly what her father had anticipated. Em had walked away from his money the day she graduated from college, and her father had often predicted she'd be back with her hand out. That had not happened, and she was determined it never would.

A small whine had Em turning to Byron, who sat at full alert, eyeing his leash hanging over the top of a file cabinet. The pup had settled in nicely, and they'd developed a routine. Walk in the morning and walk in the evening. He enjoyed sleeping on a plush blanket at the foot of her bed upstairs.

The only problem was that Byron refused to walk up or down stairs. Carrying him was a challenge, not to mention that he was a growing boy. She'd have to find time to figure out how to retrain his aversion to stairs before he had a growth spurt.

He shot her an expectant look as though he knew what time it was. The last few days, they'd walked around the block. Today, she'd take him to the park for the first time. The moment Em grabbed his leash, Byron jumped up and raced in excited circles. She flicked off the lights in the empty areas, grateful to have made it through her first week.

Locking the door, Em stepped outside into the sunshine, and

shielded her eyes with her free hand. She'd been sitting under those awful fluorescent lights way too long. A wind whooshed past, freeing leaves from the maples that lined Main Street. They danced down the sidewalk in a hurry to get somewhere.

"Let's go, Byron," Em said as she picked up her pace.

She and Byron race-walked two blocks north. Em couldn't help but smile as she passed beneath the pristine awnings of the shops. Aspen Creek seemed like a storybook town, with the unique stores lining the four blocks surrounding the town square that housed the historic courthouse and town hall right in the middle. Visitors to the San Luis Valley would be hard-pressed to ignore the quaint and friendly town.

Byron tugged on the leash and guided them to the park across from the elementary school as though he'd been there before. School had recently let out, and buses were lined up in front of the building. Laughing children ran across the park, some stopping to kick soccer balls back and forth as parents watched, chatting.

Next to the park was the dog park, a fenced-in expanse of grass surrounded by trees with benches along the perimeter. Several dog owners stood in the center of the park, throwing Frisbees and sticks for their animals to retrieve.

Large dogs. Labs, a golden retriever, and a Lassie dog. Very obedient dogs who responded immediately to commands. Byron cocked his head and solemnly observed the action as they walked past. He didn't growl, either. He watched the larger animals, his huge, brown, humanlike eyes round with awe.

"Don't worry, baby. Someday, you're going to be bigger than all of them," Em whispered to Byron.

Though the other animals were off leash, Em wasn't sure if Byron had experience with other dogs, so she kept him leashed as they jogged around the perimeter. Byron impressed her with his obedience to basic commands that hadn't interested him before.

After three laps around, though, Byron wasn't even winded. Em stopped for water. She poured some into his portable dish, then sat down and took a long swallow from her bottle.

Close by, on the next bench, a middle-aged woman smiled. Next to her, a young girl with braids intently watched the dogs, her face turned away from Em.

"What kind of dog is that?" the woman on the other bench asked.

"Byron?" Em smiled. "Vesta at the clinic tells me that he's a Bernese mountain dog and Labrador retriever mix."

"Very handsome pup."

"Thank you." Em rubbed Byron under the chin.

The girl turned around, and Em realized it was Sarah, Chase's niece.

"Sarah. Hello," Em said.

The little girl offered a shy smile.

"You've met my granddaughter?" the woman asked.

"I met Sarah at the diner this week with her uncle."

"I'm Hope Mason," the woman said. "Sarah's grandmother. I'm living in Aspen Creek for now, with Chase and Sarah."

Em worked to hide her surprise at the information. When she assessed Hope, the similarities to Chase, from the chocolate-brown hair to her hazel eyes, seemed obvious. They had the same straight nose. The only difference was the last name.

Here she was looking for an inroad to the town sheriff and one had fallen into her lap.

"Hi, Hope. I'm Emily Taylor." She kept her eye on Byron as she spoke. Sarah had inched closer and closer to him on the bench. "Nice to meet you."

"Are you new in town?"

"Can you tell?" Em smiled. "I'm the new publisher and editor of the *Aspen Creek Journal*."

"Taylor. Ah, yes. Grace mentioned you."

"Oh, you know Grace Stanton?"

"Everyone knows Grace. But she and I go way back."

"May I pet your dog?" Sarah asked.

"Well…" The literature from the vet office claimed Bernese mountain dogs were affectionate with kids.

Before Em could answer, Sarah called the dog. "Here, Byron," she said softly.

Byron ignored Em, trotted up to the little girl and put his head on her lap. Then he looked up at Sarah with bright eyes begging for attention.

"Oh my, Sarah. Look at that," the woman said. "He likes you." She turned to Em. "Sarah was very close with the neighbor's dog when she lived in Denver."

"Miss Tibbs. Yes, she told me."

The little girl put a hand on Byron's large head and gently stroked his fur. Byron closed his eyes, deeply pleased.

Em looked at Sarah, her heart aching. She was fortunate to have had such a caring grandmother. Em's father had been estranged from her only living grandparent, denying Em contact. But eventually, she'd found her grandmother herself.

"How long have you been in town?" Hope asked.

"This is my first week."

"Have you figured out how the information flows around here?"

"No," Em admitted. "I have no idea." But she'd certainly love to find out.

"Here's a little insider tidbit." Hope glanced around and then leaned closer. "The Soul Sisters."

"Soul Sisters?" That sounded like a band. Em cocked her head confused.

Hope nodded. "They know everything that's going on in town, and more times than not, the news begins with them."

"What is this? A club?"

"They're an interfaith group consisting of local women from all the churches in Aspen Creek."

"Is that right?" Em paused, thinking. This group sounded like something she needed to know more about. "How many churches are there in town?"

"Last count, five."

"I had no idea." She mulled the information. "That's a lot of churches for a town of its size."

"Yes, that's how the sisters manage to always have their finger on the pulse of the town. We meet once a month on Thursday evenings at Cora-Lee Flanagan's house. Six sharp. It's a potluck. We meet again the week after next. I'll tell her you're coming if you like."

Well, Chase's mother was a lot more helpful than he was. This was a fantastic lead, the most promising one since she'd arrived. "That would be wonderful. Thanks for the tip."

"My pleasure." She smiled. "I'd love to invite you for dinner sometime as well," Hope said. "A welcome to Aspen Creek."

Em hesitated. Somehow, she couldn't see Chase comfortable with her at his home. Their last interaction at the diner had been more than odd. Once she mentioned an interview, he'd paled and left. "I don't know… I don't want to put Chase on the spot."

Actually, she didn't mind putting the sheriff on the spot. It was her job, after all. However, his home was different, and her moral compass wouldn't allow her to leave the man without an escape route.

Hope waved a hand of dismissal. "Oh, not at all. I have friends over all the time. He's accustomed to my social tendencies, even if he is a bit of an introvert." She smiled. "Besides, Grace would be disappointed if she knew I hadn't welcomed you properly."

"Please come to dinner," Sarah said. "Bring Byron, too."

Hope's jaw sagged at her granddaughter's words. She looked at Em. "Please," she echoed. "And we'd love to have Byron. I'm sure he'd enjoy running around our backyard. Right, Sarah?"

"Oh, yes," Sarah said, her eyes bright with excitement.

Em studied the little girl, who continued to stroke Byron's fur. She had lost the momma who brushed her hair at night and whispered all the encouraging words a child needed to hear. Em swallowed. She'd do it for Sarah. If she could give the little girl a few hours of happiness with Byron, she was all in.

"All right, then. Sure. Thank you." She emptied the water in the dog dish onto the grass and shook off the moisture.

"Does next Sunday work for you?" Hope asked. "Chase is off fishing at Aspen Lake this weekend. He tells me winter comes early here, but I think he likes to hide from the world from time to time." She offered a conspiratorial smile.

Em smiled, tucking away the information about Aspen Lake. She and Chase might have more in common than she realized. Hiding from the world on occasion was a trick of hers as well.

"That would be lovely, Hope. What can I bring?"

"Just bring Byron."

"Okay. Thank you." Em gathered her things.

The little girl nodded. "Do you have to leave?"

"This is his first visit to the park," Em said. "We'll make it longer next time. I want to get him used to being social a little at a time."

"Are you keeping him?" Sarah asked, concern in her dark eyes.

"I am, unless someone claims him." Em smiled. "Maybe I'll see you the next time we walk here."

"I hope so," Sarah said softly.

"We stop by here every day after school," Hope said with a wink. "In case you ever think about giving Byron a walk at that time. We'd love to see him. And you, of course."

Sarah's eyes widened at her grandmother's words and a smile lit up her face. "We always sit on this bench."

Em chuckled at the comment. "I'll certainly bring him by when I'm able." She stood and looked at Sarah. "Sarah, it was nice to see you again."

Sarah gave a shy nod and reluctantly removed her hand from Byron.

"Lovely to meet you, Emily," Hope said. "I'll have Chase give you directions to the house."

"Thank you." Em turned and led Byron out of the park, glad that she'd run into Chase's niece and mother.

There was something about Sarah that tugged at her heart. All these years, Em had carefully guarded herself from falling in love and being hurt, but she seriously doubted she could protect herself from a sweet little girl who reminded her of her own sad childhood. And maybe she didn't want to.

Her thoughts moved to Hope, recalling the information about Chase.

Time to put her newspaper-publisher hat back on and find out exactly where Aspen Lake was located. Lakes were public, as opposed to a man's home. She needed to get started on coverage of the election campaigns, and she had zero issues with running into a candidate on public property.

Perhaps Cora-Lee Flanagan could help. Chase would not be happy to see her show up, but she had a paper to save, and this sounded like an opportunity for an exclusive feature.

Chase brought his coffee out to the small cabin's porch. He'd waited all week to head up to his fishing shack. And this week, more than any, he needed to escape. The election, Emily Taylor and the growing anxiety about the responsibility of becoming Sarah's permanent guardian weighed heavily on him. He hadn't had a decent night's sleep in days.

The cabin offered him something nothing else could. Quiet. The place held two sets of bunk beds, a scarred table that had seen its share of trout dinners, and two faux-leather, ugly-as-mud, battered brown recliners that he'd found at a yard sale.

The plain shingled cabin was one of only a few on the lake.

Most of the other structures were fancy, with all the bells and whistles of a vacation home.

Someday he'd have enough money to fix up his fishing cabin. Or maybe not. The entire one-bedroom retreat was his, and that was all that mattered. A bit weathered, the place had been around the block a few times. Like he had. It had character and withstood Colorado winters. That was all he could ask for.

This morning, as the sun rose over the mountains, Chase was once again aware of the Lord's majesty. He took a mouthful of coffee and gazed at the quiet motion of unseen energy pushing the waves in constant ripples across the lake.

Something rustled in the brush to his left, and Chase turned. He had to be hallucinating, because he was pretty sure he saw Emily Taylor's head peeking out from behind a tall cottonwood tree and a cluster of scraggly juniper shrubs. Chase checked his watch. A little after six thirty in the morning.

"Emily?"

She shoved a branch out of her way and stepped onto the dirt path leading to the cabin as though stepping onto a stage. Brushing dried needles off her sweater and jeans, she grinned at him, and he nearly expected her to curtsy and holler, "Ta-da!"

"What are you doing here? How did you even find this place?"

A moment later branches rustled again, and a huge guy, the size of a linebacker, popped his head up. Moss Boutilier wore a black woolen cap covering his shaved scalp. The long lens of his camera obscured part of his face, and a tripod was tucked under his arm. As usual, unless he wore his postal uniform, Moss was always all in black. Trademark apparel for the artistic genius. Chase had tried to have a conversation with Moss numerous times and finally given up. The man used words Chase wasn't even sure were real.

Chase grimaced. "You brought Moss?"

"He's my photographer for this piece."

"What piece?"

"Chase, I told you I want to do an in-depth interview. Show the town the real man, not simply the candidate."

"I thought you said you wanted to do a day in the life of the sheriff."

"That, too. But this is the untold story of the man behind the badge."

Rubbing the bridge of his nose, Chase took a deep breath and bit back a sharp retort. "There is no untold story."

"Everyone has a story, Chase."

He tensed. "I like my privacy, Emily."

The camera flashed, and Chase blinked and held up a hand. "Moss, what are you doing?" he said, a little stronger than intended.

Moss glowered and turned to Emily. "I cannot guarantee the structural integrity and aesthetic composition of my work if the subject fails to cooperate."

She patted the giant's massive forearm, then pinned Chase with an intense gaze. "You're doing fine. Sheriff Everett is a public figure. As such, he should be used to being in the public eye and be a little more cooperative with the press."

"Seriously, Emily? On my day off? Are you catching Buster Rutherford on his back porch in his long johns, too?"

"This is a public lake."

He waved toward the right. "The public part is down there by the water."

Emily frowned. "Well, you aren't in your long johns, and I'll have you know I conferred with your campaign manager before I made the trip out here. She assured me that this would be good for your campaign."

"Cora-Lee told you I was here?"

"No. Your mother did. However, as I said, I did check with your campaign manager first."

"You met my mother?"

"I did. She's quite lovely. Very chatty and pleasant." Emily's expression added the silent *unlike you.*

Chase groaned. Now things were starting to make sense.

"We're going to have to reschedule this little docudrama for another time. I've got fishing scheduled for this morning, and all three of us won't fit into the boat."

"If I send Moss home, may I just sit and watch you fish? Off the record."

"Off the record? I'm apparently already on the record. Moss took pictures."

"Yes, he did," she said sweetly.

He was being played, and he knew it. Yet, when he glanced from the frowning Moss to Emily, Chase found himself agreeing. "Fine."

"Thank you, Sheriff Everett. You won't even know I'm here."

"When pigs fly," he muttered.

Emily turned to Moss again. "Your work elevates the *Journal*. We both know that. Thank you so much for coming this morning. I'll be sure you're reimbursed for your time." The solicitous words were topped off with a dazzling smile.

Moss blushed. "Thank you, Emily."

Chase nearly groaned aloud as the big guy capitulated under Emily's spell. *Oh, come on.*

Emily continued her honey-eyed conversation with the photographer. "I'll talk to Cora-Lee and schedule a time to stop by the sheriff's office and get shots of him in uniform. Until then, I'll meet you at noon at Buster Rutherford's new office in town. From there, we'll go straight over to Sloane Flanagan's shop for photos."

"Yes, ma'am." Moss glared at Chase before hitching his tripod over his shoulder and turning into the brush.

"Great. Now I've broken Cora-Lee's cardinal rule," Chase said. He tossed the dregs of his coffee into a juniper bush.

"What rule is that?"

"Not to get on the wrong side of anyone before the election."

"What did you expect? You yelled at him."

"I didn't yell. I voiced my opinion louder than usual."

Emily laughed. "Maybe you should take a page from your opponent. Buster is delighted to meet with us. In fact, he's catering lunch."

"I don't want to point out the obvious, but your meeting with Buster is scheduled." He raised a palm. "This ambush was not."

"It would have been, except you've been avoiding me."

Chase stood, staring at her for several moments. He lacked the energy to muster up a snappy response. The truth was that he had been avoiding her, and he'd rather be fishing. Yet the idea of Emily tagging along was oddly as appealing as it was annoying. He was too tired to analyze that, either.

Her cell phone buzzed, and she pulled it from her back pocket. A glance at the screen changed her expression to irritation.

"Everything okay?"

"Fine. Just fine. Some people can't take no for an answer." She shoved the phone back in her pocket.

Chase nearly laughed at the irony of her words.

"So, can I stay?" Emily asked.

"As a civilian. Not as Lois Lane. I don't want to be interviewed on my day off. Besides, fishing is all about thinking. Not about talking."

"Fine." She shrugged, obviously not offended. "Got any more coffee?"

"Sure." He turned and moved up the steps.

He heard her footfall on the wooden steps as she followed behind.

"Can you fish?" he asked.

"I don't want to shock you, but yes, I can fish."

He held open the door and met her gaze. "Is that right?"

"I had a nanny who took me fishing all the time."

"A nanny?"

"Nanny. Babysitter. Whatever." Emily glanced around the cabin and, to her credit, never once grimaced at the interior. "Rustic," she finally said.

"That's not what most people say, but thanks."

He headed to the tiny kitchen and poured coffee into a mug. Black, as he recalled from the diner. "Here you go."

She inhaled the coffee aroma, sipped and nodded with approval. "Very good on the details there, Sheriff."

"They pay me to pay attention to details."

"Oh, and thank you for the beautiful welcome plant."

"The sheriff's department sent that."

"Yes. Of course." She sipped the coffee again and set it on the counter.

He looked at her before opening a closet. "I only have one pole here at the moment."

"I'm not here to fish." She clasped her hands together, hesitating for a moment. "Look, I know my showing up here seems self-serving, but this isn't about me. It's about the *Journal*."

"What about the paper?"

"Chase—" She paused, distress in her eyes. "If I don't get things turned around, the paper is going to go under."

If what she said was true, it was not good. "The *Journal* has been around as long as the town, they tell me," he replied.

"That may be true, but the paper's circulation has decreased to near pitiful. Advertising is down. Grace has had other, more pressing things on her mind. Things have quietly slid out of control." She bit her lip and then continued. "The citizens of Aspen Creek are reading the *Paradise Gazette* for news and entertainment. That's discouraging."

"Ah, so now I see why you're here. You want to flatter me into helping you." He took a pole and tackle box from the closet and put them near the door.

She scoffed. "That's not it at all. I'm here first and foremost because you're eye candy. You'll sell papers."

Chase's head jerked up at the last words. "Eye *what*? Is that a joke?"

"Surely you look in the mirror on occasion. You're single and handsome. You wear a uniform with a badge and a cowboy hat. All women swoon over that stuff."

"All women?" He narrowed his eyes and met her gaze. Was he imagining it or was Emily Taylor blushing?

"Most women."

Chase offered a harrumph at her response and handed her his pole. "You can assist me today since you don't have a license. Be careful with the pole. It's my favorite."

"I will." She looked the pole up and down and paused. "Um, Chase, about the interview?"

"How about if you forget about the interview for today and instead, I offer a trade."

"A trade."

"Maybe you'd like to do a ride-along, sometime. For the *Journal*. I'll also give Moss access to the office for photos."

"What's the catch?" She narrowed her eyes.

"Quid pro quo. I give you what you need, and you give me what I need. I'm offering a ride-along and am availing the office for a photo session."

"Quid pro quo?" Emily's frown deepened, as did the suspicion that laced her voice. "What do you want in return?"

"I want my personal life and my family off-limits."

She sighed. "Okay."

"Great. Monday morning work for you for the ride-along?"

"Sure."

"Come on," Chase said. "I'm running late if I want to catch my lunch."

"Yes, sir."

"We'll go down to the end of the dock. I've got a small boat there."

He frowned, assessing her dark slacks and sweater. "I'll grab a life vest. You have sunscreen on?"

"I hadn't planned to do anything requiring sunscreen, and it's barely sixty degrees." She frowned. "And I do not need a life vest. I'm an experienced swimmer."

"Fine, but the elevation is almost eight thousand feet above sea level. It's easy to burn up, no matter the temperature." He tossed her a plastic bottle, dug in the closet and pulled out a life vest.

"I said I can swim," she said.

"You wear the vest or you wait on the dock." He shrugged.

"Fine." She gritted out the word before finishing off her coffee and putting the mug in the sink.

Chase grabbed the plastic cooler from the kitchen table and picked up the tackle box before elbowing open the screen door. "Follow me."

In the distance, birds chirped and a flock of sandhill cranes soared across the sky, migrating to New Mexico for the upcoming winter. Around them, the golden leaves of the aspens glowed against the blue sky. Tall conifers formed a tree line guiding them along the path from his front door to the community pier, where the sun-dappled water welcomed them.

"How long have you been in Aspen Creek this time?" Emily asked.

Chase blinked and slowly turned his head toward his companion.

"What?" Emily murmured. "I'm making conversation."

"Is this conversation on the record?" Chase returned. He kept walking.

"Do you have something to hide?" she asked.

He stiffened at the words, eyes on the stony trail. "I'm sure I have as many secrets as you do."

"I don't have secrets," she scoffed.

"Emily, everyone has secrets." Some tore families apart, and others, like his, drew them together. He wouldn't have made it through that dark season so long ago without the support of his mother and little sister. Chase would do anything for his family.

They reached the pier, where the sound of their footsteps echoed on the wooden planks. "You're okay with boats?"

"You mean that?" She nodded toward his small red fishing boat tied to the right of the pier. "That isn't a boat. It's a canoe. But to answer your question, I'm fine with boats. I rowed in college."

"That so?" He took in the information. She had a nanny and rowed in college. Funny, he'd never put all the pieces of the puzzle that was Emily together before. For a moment, Chase was taken back to Emily's first arrival in Aspen Creek. Grace had been so thrilled, she shared with everyone that her young intern was from an Ivy League college.

Not that her background mattered. It only reinforced what he knew to be true, then and now: They had little in common. They'd never actually chatted much the last time she was in town, either. He'd recognized his attraction right away and kept his distance. Despite that, she'd continued to seek him out.

Now, twelve years later, the attraction remained, but this time Emily's interest in him was strictly about leveraging him to sell papers. A good thing, he reminded himself.

Body low, he grabbed the closest gunnel, stepped into the boat and grabbed the other gunnel. "Mind handing me that stuff?" He nodded toward the cooler, tackle box and rod on the dock. Once he'd placed the equipment in the boat for balance, he held his hand out to Emily. She took it and, crouching down, stepped into the boat.

Chase mentally amended his assessment as he held her hand. *Nothing in common except an annoying chemistry.*

"All good?" he asked, once she'd settled near the bow.

Emily nodded, not looking directly at him.

"Wasn't expecting company, so I only have one paddle," he said. "But we aren't going out far. We could easily swim back to shore."

"Works for me."

When they reached a reasonable distance from the dock, Chase eased up from his knees and sat on the bench.

"Now I'm going to concentrate on the fish and try not to think about the fact that you're here doing your best to get a story while pretending you're not trying to get a story."

"I'm also interested in getting to know Chase Everett better," she said softly.

"Are you?" Chase glanced at her.

Her brown hair glinted in the morning sunlight, the lighter strands golden as she met his gaze. "Yes. Aren't we friends?"

"Are we?"

Emily frowned. "Stop that."

"Stop what?"

"Asking me a question every time I ask you a question."

Chase hid a smile and didn't answer as he opened the tackle box. He prepped his line, then carefully cast it onto the water.

"So, how long did you say you've been back in town?" Emily persisted.

"That's public knowledge. Four and a half years."

"What brought you?"

"I was working in Denver when I got a call that Sheriff Flanagan passed. The town council members asked me to come and interview. The interview took twenty minutes. They pinned a badge on me before the hour was out. No one else wanted the job. So, here I am."

"This has to be a career step down for you."

"Don't move." Chase nodded across the lake to where a deer slipped between two large maples and stepped up to the shore for a drink. The sunlight between the trees dappled across the scene. "Can you hold my line for a second so I can snap a picture?" he whispered.

"Sure. Could you take one with my phone as well?"

"I can do that."

Emily dug in her pocket and handed him her phone.

Chase snapped her picture. As he finished, the phone in his hand began to vibrate. He took the pole from her and handed over the cell. "I guess you better take this."

Emily glanced at the screen and sighed as she stuffed the phone in her pocket. "Thanks. Not important."

He nodded at the words, returned the pole to her and snapped his own pictures of the deer. Chase snuck a look at Emily. Maybe not important, but that call seemed to have rattled her a bit.

"Uh-oh." Eyes rounding, Emily inhaled sharply. "Something's pulling on your line." She started to shift in the boat.

"No," he commanded. "Sit still. I have it on good authority that this is a tippy canoe. I've overturned it a few times myself."

Still, Emily struggled with the line. Her arm jerked back, her elbow striking his hand with force. Chase's phone flipped into the air. The cell sailed through the air and splashed into the water with a loud *kerplunk*, only to be swallowed by the lake.

For a moment, he stared at the spot where his phone had disappeared in disbelief.

"I thought you'd been fishing before," he finally said.

"I'm so sorry," Emily said softly. "I have fished, but it was a long time ago." She continued to grip the pole tightly.

He slowly inched toward her, maintaining the boat's balance, took the rod and reeled in the line. Like his phone, the bait was gone and the fish was nowhere in sight.

Chase sighed.

"I feel terrible. I'll pay for your phone."

"Not necessary. This gives me a good excuse to go without

one for the weekend. There's an emergency burner in the cabin and my mother knows where to find me."

Emily nodded, her face reflecting misery. Now he felt bad. It was an accident, and he had a feeling there would be more when a journalist was around. Maybe he ought to get used to it.

"I should use this time to interview you," Chase said. "Since you're stuck in a boat with me."

A small smile touched her lips.

"So you've been living in Denver until recently?"

"Denver has always been my home base, even when I was traveling." She paused, seeming to measure her words. "I didn't know I had a grandmother until after college. I tracked her down, and since then I've come home to Denver as much as possible to spend time with her."

"Didn't know you had a grandmother? One who lived in Denver? How'd that happen?"

"It's complicated."

"Yeah, family usually is." He nodded.

"True. Which reminds me, I ran into your mother and Sarah at the park. Hope said she was visiting from Denver herself. Her last name is different than yours?"

Chase looked at her. Right…she'd met his mom. That couldn't be good. He took a deep breath. As much as he hated talking about himself, maybe if he explained to Emily she'd back off. He couldn't stand it if his family's tragedy was on display to sell papers or to further his career.

"Ah, yeah. My father passed when I was in middle school. She remarried." He paused and glanced away. "Didn't last."

Emily nodded.

"Anyhow, my mother is helping me get my niece settled in." He stared out across the water. "We lost my sister last year." His gut clenched as he thought about Phoebe. Chase turned to Emily. "I don't want you to put my family in any article you write."

Dismay shot across her face. "I already agreed not to. Besides, give me some credit. I do have principles." Brows scrunched together with concern, she met his gaze. "I'm very sorry for your loss."

"Thanks. It's been a rough year, and I guess I'm a little defensive."

"As you should be."

He nodded and sneaked a peek at Emily. She had a hand in the water. With that musing smile on her face, she looked for all the world as if she belonged in this particular spot at this particular moment in time.

In a heartbeat, Chase realized he meant the words, which was a little worrisome, as the woman had been in Aspen Creek less than a week. His gut told him that it was very important that he stay a step ahead of the inquisitive journalist.

They sat quietly for a few minutes, and Chase realized he wasn't going to catch a thing as long as Emily was here. No self-respecting fish would go anywhere near his line while she was moving her hand in the water. Good thing he had brought groceries. Tomorrow was another day.

Chapter Five

"Did he get my good side?" Buster Rutherford asked, a hand on his ample girth. He glanced in the mirror across from his massive cherrywood desk and gave a self-satisfied nod at his reflection in a bespoke striped suit.

Moss growled as he put away his equipment.

"I'm not sure you have a side that isn't good, sir." Em appraised the candidate with a slow glance. At six feet tall, Buster was a well-padded—physically and financially—ambulance chaser with a poor reputation in his chosen field. Remaining unbiased for this piece would be a challenge when everything she'd researched pointed to a shady character.

The candidate offered a deep belly laugh. "Well done. You should be a politician, young lady."

"Oh, no. I'm happy simply delivering the news to the good citizens of Aspen Creek."

"How do you like being a reporter for the *Journal*?" he asked as he moved behind his desk and slid into a large chair resembling a leather throne. Buster offered a sweep of his hand. "Please, do sit."

Emily turned to her photographer. "Moss, you can go ahead. Will you please email Harley and let her know that I want Mr. Rutherford's picture above the fold? I'll meet you at the tea shop…" She glanced at her watch. "In an hour."

Moss glared at Buster before nodding. He heaved the equipment over his shoulder, his expression dark.

If possible, Buster's ego swelled even larger at Em's words. "Front and center. That's what I want to hear, and so will the mayor. Thank you, Ms. Taylor."

Em smiled politely and sat down in one of the leather chairs on the other side of the desk. She glanced around. Buster had transformed an empty storefront around the corner from the Aspen Creek courthouse into campaign headquarters, complete with an impressive office.

"I'm the publisher and editor in chief. I own the paper," Em replied. "Following Grace Stanton's legacy is an honor and a challenge."

"What happened to Grace Stanton?" he asked.

"Ms. Stanton retired," Emily said.

"Why would a smart, and if you don't mind my stating the obvious, beautiful woman like yourself want to own a small-town paper?"

Em tried not to roll her eyes. This wasn't the first time someone subtly challenged her credentials. She had rushed home from Aspen Lake and changed into a gray suit, hoping to start out on the right foot with the attorney. Now, as it turned out, Buster was simply another politician who patted her on the head.

"I'm a journalist. I have a degree." *From an Ivy League school my father insisted I attend.* "And I've covered stories all over the world, from Buenos Aires to South Africa."

"That so?" He shook his head. "Still, I thought newspapers were dead. Isn't the internet the new communication tool? Don't all you young people do everything on your phone?"

"I can see how you might believe that's the norm, since it's somewhat true in cities and suburbs. However, it does not necessarily apply to many small towns across America, especially in rural areas with limited internet and cell coverage. The demographics of small rural towns include twenty-two percent of folks over sixty-five, and those people like the feel of paper in their hands. But we do have a web version of the *Journal* available. That aside, sir, if run correctly, the local weekly paper is surviving and thriving."

There was no need to share that their particular weekly was on the struggle bus.

"Thriving? How can that be?" He frowned, confused. "The *Journal* is ten pages at best."

"We're a weekly, for one. The weekly doesn't try to be anything except what it is, a document of life in Aspen Creek. No big-city paper is going to cover that. They don't care. We at the *Journal* care. Our ten pages reflect the heart of this town."

"You speak as though you're a native."

"Do I?" She smiled, inordinately pleased at his words. "I like to pretend I am. I'm here to stay, so eventually, I'm hoping folks will forget the day I arrived and consider me part of the scenery."

Buster fiddled with a glass trophy on his desk. She could practically hear the gears in his head grinding. The man seemed determined to challenge her at every turn.

"I heard a rumor the paper was on its last legs."

Uh-oh, the rumor mill had already begun. She had to nip that in the bud, fast, and create confidence in the *Journal*. "We're in…transition as we move from one publisher's vision to the next adventure. I'm certain the citizens of Aspen Creek will be delighted with our plans."

He eyed her with skepticism. "And why is it you interviewed Everett first, might I ask?"

"Sir, I'm doing a series of articles on both candidates. And he is the incumbent, isn't he?"

"Hmm, I heard you two went fishing." He raised his brows. "Not exactly unbiased reporting."

"I'm sure you understand that sometimes our business and professional lives overlap. After all, you are the mayor's nephew." She leaned forward. "However, you were misinformed. He fished. I asked questions." Em took a calming breath, alarmed that Buster knew she was on Aspen Lake this morning. She didn't like the way he'd mentioned it, either.

Buster had no response.

"Well, I don't want to overstay my welcome," Emily said. "Thank you for lunch and the opportunity to get to know you, Mr. Rutherford."

"My pleasure. Good to get to know you as well, Ms. Taylor. As the next sheriff of Aspen Creek, I believe you and I should have a strong working relationship."

Em chuckled. "Sir, the election is still weeks away. But let me ask, why sheriff?"

"It doesn't take much to manage a Podunk sheriff's department." He shrugged. "I'm an attorney. I know the law."

"Podunk?" She cocked her head. "Is that your platform, sir?"

Buster blustered. "No. That's off the record. I'm here because the Rutherfords have a history in Aspen Creek. We care about this town."

"Mr. Rutherford, do you mind if I ask you a few final questions? On the record."

"Of course not. I'm all about transparency."

"Last month, the *Denver Post* published a claim that your firm in Denver is about to be investigated by the FCC for insider trading." She wouldn't print that in the paper. It was old news, and her goal was not to show bias nor to sling mud. But she did want to make Buster aware that she was informed.

There was no mistaking the second of panic that flashed across Buster's face before he composed himself.

"If you'd done your homework, you'd know that it is no longer my firm. I turned in my resignation in order to run for office here in Aspen Creek unencumbered." He dismissed her words with a wave of a meaty hand and a blustery sound that all but said, *move along, nothing to see here.*

"Yes, sir, I understand. The *Post*, however, is specifically naming one of your clients as a source. They allege that a federal indictment may be forthcoming. Are you concerned that you might be subpoenaed?"

"Now, you know I can't discuss anything that has to do with my clients." He narrowed his eyes. "What's happening at my former firm has nothing to do with me. So if you're looking for dirt, you'll have to look elsewhere."

She wasn't looking for dirt, but she couldn't ignore her research, either.

Emily nodded slowly. "Again, I appreciate your time." When she stood and offered her hand, it was swallowed in his large one.

Buster's beady-eyed gaze met hers. "I'll be sure you have a ringside table at my fund-raising dinner for full coverage in the *Journal*."

Emily slipped her fingers from his clammy hand and reached for her tote. "Thank you, sir."

"Ms. Taylor?"

She looked up.

"While I appreciate your thorough reporting, I hope you're checking into Sheriff Everett as thoroughly as you seem to be checking into me. You never know what you might find."

"Yes, sir. I am."

A phone rang, and Buster pulled a cell from his pocket. "If you will excuse me?"

Emily nodded and turned to leave. Rutherford's words followed her as she stepped out into the sunshine and glanced around Main Street. *You never know what you might find...* She found the words suspect.

However, she'd barely started her research on the candidates. Was Buster feeding her political rhetoric in an attempt to keep her attention elsewhere? Either way, part of her job meant trusting her gut, and her gut said Chase was on the up and up.

However, Buster was correct about one thing: It was her responsibility to investigate both candidates. Complete, truthful and unbiased investigation. That was her job as publisher and editor of the *Journal*. No matter how her stomach fluttered around Chase Everett.

"You what?" Chase nearly dropped the jar of jam in his hand. He placed the container on the counter next to the peanut butter and turned to look at his mother, seated at the kitchen table, serenely dropping bombs on his Monday morning.

Hope took a sip of her coffee, carefully placed the cup in the saucer and smiled. "I invited Emily Taylor to dinner on Sunday. I'm thinking my pot roast and homemade rolls. I'll whip up some chive butter to go along. Maybe that lemon cream cheese icebox cake for dessert. What are your thoughts?"

He stared at her for a moment, but unlike most of the folks in town, his mother was neither impressed nor intimidated by his uniform or his icy glare. She simply smiled again and adjusted the sweater around her shoulders. An early riser like himself, she was dressed for the day, though she could have slept in. It was his responsibility to make Sarah's lunch and take her to school in the mornings. A responsibility he enjoyed. The short drive to the elementary school offered an opportunity to ask questions and slowly draw Sarah out of her shell.

"Why would you do that?" he finally asked. And why did Emily Taylor keep popping up in his life? First at the lake on Saturday, then there was today's ride-along, and now dinner on Sunday.

"Emily is new to town, and it's customary to be welcoming and hospitable to newcomers."

Chase spread jam on one side of the wheat bread and the peanut butter on another slice before putting them together and cutting the sandwich into four neat triangles with pristine edges.

That was the way Phoebe had always done it for Sarah. Consistency, the therapist reminded him, was important.

Sarah walked into the room, carrying her backpack, her long dark hair pulled back into that strange braid on the back of her head. His mother's handiwork. So far, he was a failure in the hair department.

"Byron is coming, too," Sarah said. She peeked at the sandwich on the cutting board and gave a small nod of approval before dropping her backpack on the floor and claiming a chair at the kitchen table. Those little nods made his day, giving him hope that he'd eventually master parenthood.

A pretty yellow checkerboard tablecloth that Chase had never seen in his life adorned the table where his mother had already set out Sarah's bowl, spoon and juice glass. He glanced around his once-plain kitchen. Not only had she hired a decorator, but every day his mother added a few more homey touches that made his house look less like a hotel.

"Who's Byron?" he asked his niece.

Sarah turned and looked at him as though he wasn't very bright. "Byron is Emily's dog. I played with him at the park Friday." She frowned. "You were gone fishing."

Guilty. Maybe he should take Sarah fishing sometime like his mother had suggested. An image of himself, Sarah and Emily in the boat flashed through his mind and he smiled, then dismissed it.

"I guess you like Byron?" he asked, eager to pursue any topic that had Sarah talking.

"Yes," she said. "I like Emily, too." She reached for the box of her favorite cereal, waiting on the table, and poured the fat flakes into her bowl.

Chase quickly grabbed milk from the fridge and held it over her bowl. "Tell me when," he said and started pouring.

Sarah put up a hand. "When. Thank you, Uncle Chase."

"So, Sarah, why do you like Emily?" he continued.

"She smiles a lot, and she's pretty and nice." His niece shrugged and stirred her cereal.

Chase's eyes widened. The kid told it like she saw it. And it was the truth, he admitted silently.

His mother cleared her throat and shot him a knowing look.

"And what about Byron?" Chase asked. "What kind of dog is he?"

Sarah looked at her grandmother.

"Bernese mountain and Labrador mix," Hope said.

"That kind," Sarah replied. She dug into her cereal and began to study the back of the box. Conversation over.

Chase put the milk in the fridge and eyed his mother.

"Okay, so it looks like Byron and Emily are coming to dinner on Sunday. Good call, Mother."

Hope dipped her head in acknowledgment. "I thought so."

Now all he had to do was make very certain that Emily left her press pass at the front door.

An hour later, Chase slid into the driver's seat of his official Aspen Creek Sheriff's Department patrol vehicle and turned to Emily. She smiled a little too eagerly as she placed her tablet on her lap.

"A few ground rules," he said. "Wear the vest at all times and stay in the vehicle unless I deem it's safe to get out."

Emily tugged at the Kevlar. "This isn't exactly comfortable."

"It's for your protection, and you'll only be with me a short time. Thus, only wearing the vest for a short time."

"Do you mind sharing the last time bullets flew in Aspen Creek?"

"Good question. Not since I've been here. We have a few notable rabble-rousers who routinely give us a reason to keep our two jail cells clean and ready for occupancy, but so far no weapons issues."

She scoffed with outrage. "Then why am I wearing a bulletproof vest?"

"This town has a total of four gun shops, but only one grocery store. Our citizens take their Second Amendment rights more seriously than their avocados."

"That doesn't answer my question."

Chase released a breath. The woman was unyielding. "Because although Cora-Lee says our insurance covers a civilian in the vehicle, I'm not convinced that's correct. You're wearing a vest because I'm not taking any chances and because I prefer you alive and annoying."

"There's a compliment I haven't come across." She grinned. "I'll take it, Sheriff. Thank you."

"Seat belt on at all times as well," he muttered.

"Yes, sir."

He stared at her from across the vehicle. "You may call me 'Sheriff,' but 'sir' is over the top."

"Yes, Sheriff." Emily nodded. "May I ask questions?"

"Yeah, but everything is off the record unless we agree it's not, and no video or audio recording."

"That's not helpful." She frowned. "You're a civil servant, and everything you do is public record. You even wear a camera whose footage is available to the public per the Freedom of Information Act."

"That may be, but we don't do things in Aspen Creek like they do in big cities. We respect the privacy of our citizens. If you want camera footage, fill out the appropriate FOIA forms available at the town hall."

"This isn't about me coming out to the lake, is it? I'm so sorry about your phone."

"I've got a replacement on the way." Chase slipped his sunglasses on. "But, no. It's not about the lake."

"Good," she said. "Because information gathering is my job, Sheriff, and I do my job well."

He fastened his seat belt. Yes, she did. A little too well.

"So your job on patrol is to sit here all day until something happens?" Emily asked.

"You're kidding, right?" Chase chuckled and started the vehicle. "My job is to patrol the town. This vehicle is a powerful deterrent. I want it to be seen, and I don't mean getting doughnuts."

"I didn't mean…"

He grinned. "I'm just giving you a hard time. Let's ride around." Chase signaled and checked his mirrors before pulling into traffic.

"May I inquire why Aspen Creek has a sheriff's department as opposed to a police department? Do you ride horses, too?"

"You sure know the hot-button question to ask." He raised a hand to wave at a delivery guy in a brown truck parked outside the Fashion Boutique on the other side of the barbershop.

"I'll take that as a compliment." She scribbled on the pad again. "Goodness, two compliments before noon. This is turning out to be a stellar Monday."

Chase cleared his throat. "The answer to your question is very simple. Mayor Vernon Rutherford. County law enforcement have the historic title of sheriff and we're the police. Our mayor likes the concept of a sheriff and deputies to enhance the flavor of Aspen Creek as a Western tourist town, so he petitioned and got it on the ballot years ago." He shot her a quick glance. "Off the record, the other sheriff's departments no doubt laugh when they drive through town."

"That's unfortunate."

"It is what it is. Their jurisdiction is the entire county. Ours is Aspen Creek."

Em nodded.

"We're sitting in the middle of one of the biggest tourist destinations in the area. Folks come through hunting, fly-fishing, hiking and camping. In the winter, there's a variety of snow activities. Not to mention the Great Sand Dunes National Park is only an hour away." Chase shrugged. "If cowboy hats and boots keep us relevant, that's fine by me."

After a beat, she looked up. "Who dispatches law enforcement, ambulance and fire for Aspen Creek?"

"I get nonemergency calls directly from Cora-Lee during the week until 5:00 p.m. After-hours calls and all emergency calls are dispatched out of Alamosa. The same with ambulance service. We have our own volunteer fire department, and they're also dispatched completely out of Alamosa."

For minutes, she was silent, peering at the screen of his mobile laptop and assessing the patrol car's dashboard. He found himself relieved when her questions detoured to weapons and the law, something he enjoyed talking about.

Silence stretched as he drove up and down the residential streets of Aspen Grove. "How are things going at the *Journal*?"

"That's a challenging question. I did get a lead from your mother. I'm attending the Soul Sisters meeting next Thursday."

Chase cringed. "Aw, why would you do that?"

"Hope says they're a great source of information on the inner workings of the town."

He pulled up to a red light on Main and stopped. Amy from the diner crossed the street and gave him a wave. Chase gave a toot of the horn in response, and she laughed.

"Did my mother also mention that if you aren't careful, they'll have you assigned to half a dozen projects in your spare time?"

"That's not going to happen because I don't have any spare time. I'll barely have enough time to swing by the park with Byron in the afternoons to visit Sarah once or twice this week."

"You're going to do that?" He stared at her for a moment.

"I'm going to do my best."

"That's really nice of you." Maybe he'd jumped to way too many conclusions about Emily. In Sarah's words, Emily was a nice person who smiled a lot and happened to be pretty.

"Don't sound so surprised, Chase. I am a nice person."

"Well, nice person, my advice to you is to learn to say no before you attend the Soul Sisters meeting. Practice in a mirror."

Emily scoffed. "I think you're exaggerating."

"I'm not. Those ladies are a force, and that is not a compliment."

"But your mother attends."

"She's merely a visiting minion. Since she was diagnosed and completed her cancer treatment, they don't pressure her to participate in their world-domination plans."

Emily released a small gasp. "Your mother is a cancer survivor? Oh, my. What a difficult time for your family."

"Yeah, it's been challenging. The thing about my mother is she's always upbeat. Turns everything over to the Lord." Chase paused. "I am constantly inspired by her faith."

"Wow, you're fortunate to have her in your life."

He nodded. "I couldn't agree more."

They were silent for minutes as Chase drove through the back roads of town and circled back to Main Street. He sneaked a look at Emily and then focused on the road again, once again considering the possibility that he'd judged her prematurely. Perhaps she didn't have an agenda 24-7. He'd like to believe that maybe this time around, they could be friends. Maybe more.

"I received the invitation to your campaign dinner," Emily finally said.

"When is that?" He turned on to Aspen Leaf and drove toward the elementary school. Chase made it a habit to drive by the two schools in town a couple of times a day.

"You don't know?"

"I've put it out of my head."

"It's a week from this Saturday."

"That soon? I guess I'll be there, too." Whether he liked it or not.

"Good plan." Emily chuckled. "It will be a great story for the paper. We need more great stories." She sighed. "Nothing happens in Aspen Creek. Not like in Paradise. Have you read their paper? The police blotter section of the *Gazette* is a hit."

"I don't think emulating the *Gazette* is the best plan." He glanced at her again. "I've been giving your problem some thought."

"Which problem?"

"The low circulation stats."

"Oh! Well, I'm honored and shocked that you'd give the paper your attention."

"What about an open house at the *Journal* offices? Make it easy for the community to get to know you and offer their input for the paper?"

"Yes. Yes. A terrific idea. Thank you."

Emily typed on her tablet, a smile on her face. Chase liked that smile. Liked that he'd put it there, and he'd like to do it more often. But was it possible for him to be an ordinary guy, enjoying the company of a woman, without his past constantly overshadowing?

"So, you and your dog are coming to dinner on Sunday," Chase said. "When were you going to mention that?"

"I wasn't going to. That's Hope's job." Emily peeked at him. "Are you okay with the invitation?"

"Sarah is, and that's all that matters."

Emily blinked and stared at him. "If you don't want me to come to dinner, say so. I can arrange another time for Sarah to visit with Byron."

He grimaced at his tactless response. Here his niece was excited and anticipating Emily and her dog's visit, and he was grousing like a grump.

"I apologize. I'm a little stressed these days. I'm delighted to have you and your dog visit my humble abode."

"Delighted? I doubt. But why stressed?"

Chase hesitated. Maybe it would be a good idea to tell Emily what was on the line. Could he trust her with the information? He prayed so.

"Off the record?" he asked.

"Sure."

"It's been nearly a year since my sister, Phoebe, passed. Sarah is only starting to settle in, and as you probably noticed, she's still very introverted." He looked at Emily.

"I totally understand. I lost my own mother at her age." Her lips thinned and she nodded solemnly.

Chase jerked back at her words and ran a hand over his mouth. "I… I wasn't aware. I'm sorry for that."

"I'm telling you because I know what Sarah is going through. I get it, and I won't do anything to mess up the balance you've established."

"Thank you." Perhaps that was why Sarah connected with Emily. She sensed her empathy.

"That's why the election is so important for you," she said.

"Yeah, that's right," he said, surprised at her response. "More importantly, I have petitioned the court to adopt Sarah. I need everything to be in order come November when we have the social worker evaluation and go before the judge."

"What makes you think there will be problems?" she asked.

"If I lose the election, I'd be unemployed until I applied for another position in Denver or maybe Alamosa. That would mean a move. A scenario that isn't ideal for Sarah." His niece grieved quietly, and the therapist had emphasized the importance of continuity in her daily life. Moving would destroy the safe space he and his mother had worked so hard to create for her and could set her back months.

"I see," Emily said. She looked at him for a long moment. "You're a good uncle, Chase Everett."

Chase considered her words. Not a day went by that he didn't pray and ask the good Lord to show him how to be the guardian his niece needed and deserved. The parent that his sister would want him to be. "Thanks," he finally said.

They drove the streets surrounding the town square, where a few people walked their dogs in the September sunshine. Maples and aspens surrounding the square fluttered in the breeze, their amber and gold leaves shimmering.

Chase smiled. "Byron, huh?"

"Vesta at the clinic named him. He's a Labernese."

"I heard. That's a new one on me."

"Me, too. Byron and Sarah definitely have a connection."

"I'm glad. She wants a dog, but I don't think I can take on one more thing right now."

"That's what I said before Byron showed up. Now I'm praying no one claims him." She shrugged. "Sometimes good things happen when you least expect it and when you think you can't possibly manage one more thing in your life. And sometimes, they end up being the missing piece in your life."

Chase turned his head for a moment, catching the earnest expression on her face. Perhaps there was some wisdom to her words. Could his life get any busier than it was now? And a dog might be exactly what Sarah needed. He would absolutely pray about the situation.

"Thanks, I'll keep that in mind," he said. "I appreciate your input."

Emily smiled, and he detected a blush on her cheeks. "Happy to help. I'll be praying for things to slow down for you."

"Aw, I might have exaggerated. I do believe things are looking up."

"Are they?"

Chase looked at Emily and realized the truth of his words. "Yeah, they are." In the week since Emily had arrived, life had definitely improved. He couldn't deny the attraction to the journalist, nor how his day brightened when she appeared.

If he managed to keep the lid on his past, maybe he could give a little more thought to his future. For the first time in a long time, he felt a glimmer of something that looked like hope. The fact that that hope included Emily was both unexpected and a little terrifying.

Chapter Six

"*Voici votre courrier, chères dames*," Moss called as he strode into the *Journal* offices and stepped into the conference room. This week, his cravat was bright blue, and he'd added a French beret at a jocular angle. Still not exactly official postal uniform accessories, but they suited Moss. He tugged a leather mail satchel off his shoulder and offered a sweeping bow.

"*Merci*, Moss," Em returned.

"Stop that," Harley said from behind him. "I took Spanish in high school and failed."

"Apologies," Moss said to Harley. "I said, 'here's the mail.'"

Em laughed as she took the stack of mail he handed her. "Have you heard anything?"

"Heard anything?" He narrowed his eyes in question.

"It's Friday. The paper has been out since Tuesday. Even the subscribers should have their copy now." Em could barely contain her excitement. "Surely you've heard people talking."

"About what?" Moss asked.

"Moss! My editorial, or the new advice column."

"*Dispatches from the Heart?*" He shook his head and rolled his eyes, making his opinion on the name of the column clear. "No, but you have to give it a while."

"What's a while mean? I haven't even gotten an email in response."

"Emily, change is slow in this town. You know that, right?" Harley said softly from the doorway.

"Sure. Right. Of course." Em sighed and started to sort the mail.

"Are we still on for that interview with the principal of the high school on Monday?" Moss asked.

"It's on my calendar," Em said.

"Excellent. I've attended the football team's practice and have obtained prodigious photos for next week's paper. I'll deliver them when I have completed my appointed rounds this afternoon."

"Prodigious, huh?"

"Adjective. Meaning remarkably impressive."

Em laughed. "I know what it means, and yes, you are."

"Thank you so much." Moss bowed. "And what about the sheriff?" he asked.

"Oh, that. I'll call Cora-Lee, and we'll schedule a photo shoot in his office next week. Hopefully on Monday as well."

He nodded and hoisted the leather mail pouch onto his shoulder. "Emily?"

"Yes?" She looked up.

"Cheer up. You're doing an extraordinary job. You are a woman with vision. I'm honored to work with you," Moss said. He turned and headed out of the office.

"He's right, Emily," Harley chimed in. "You've been here two weeks, and you've already moved mountains. Tomorrow is Saturday. Relax and forget about the paper until Monday."

"If only I could forget about the paper," Em said. She looked at Harley. "You added the open house information to next week's edition, right?"

"Yes, and it's an excellent idea, by the way."

"I can't take credit for it. Chase dropped it in my lap during the ride-along."

"Is that right?" Harley eyed her from the doorway. "*Chase.* You're on a first-name basis already?"

"Not already. Chase and I met twelve years ago here in Aspen Creek when I was an intern at the paper. So, yes, we are on a first-name basis."

"That explains a lot," Harley murmured as she exited the room.

Hmm. Em didn't like that gleam in her managing editor's eye. She and Chase were colleagues, acquaintances. Some days, she thought they were friends. But nothing more, though the idea of something more with Chase had danced through her thoughts at odd moments. Like when he looked at her intently with those hazel eyes. She pushed the wayward thoughts away. Definitely not in her five-year plan.

Returning to the job at hand, Em shuffled through a stack of envelopes. Bills on the bottom, everything else on top. She fought a niggle of despair at the realization that there was a lot on the bottom of the pile.

"Anything interesting?" Harley asked. She wandered back into the room with a coffee mug in her hand and glanced out the big window.

"Not so far." Em held up a plain white business envelope, postmarked Aspen Creek with no return address, and slid her finger under the gummed flap. Her eyes rounded as she read the contents. "Oh, my," she said with a laugh.

Harley moved closer. "What is it?"

"Listen.

"Dear *Dispatches from the Heart*,
You've got it all wrong. In your advice to Single in Aspen Creek, you suggest that she stop being a basset hound. Make herself unavailable to get her man to notice her.

I disagree. Women and men need to base their relationships on honesty. You're encouraging dishonesty.

Sincerely,
An honest man."

"Our first letter." Harley squealed. "Who's it from?"

"I have no idea." Em examined the envelope once more. "The postmark is Aspen Creek. That's all there is. Obviously, he wants to remain anonymous, or he'd have sent an email."

"What are you going to do?"

"Answer, of course. Especially since our anonymous correspondent did a nice job twisting my words around. Our columnist will respond to that as well."

Harley chuckled. "Which columnist would that be?"

"No one needs to know it's me."

"You may start a firestorm," Harley returned.

"That's what I'm hoping. A firestorm of readers." Em grinned and tucked the letter away. This was good news. Readers were engaging and responding. She couldn't ask for anything better.

Harley strolled to the big front window once again, glanced up and down the street, and sighed.

"How's it going with Ryan?" Em asked.

"Ugh. It's been torture. I don't think I would have made it if not for these windows that let me peek into downtown."

"Is our plan working?"

"Your plan," Harley corrected. She sighed again. "I don't know. I love my ceramics class, so that's a plus. And Andy Pickering, the head librarian, has been flirting."

"Is that a good thing?"

"Andy is no Murphy, but he's cute in a nerdy, bookish sort of way. A girl does like to be appreciated."

"Having choices is empowering. I'm sure Ryan will catch on soon and appreciate the change in you."

"I sure hope so." She looked at Em. "Have you ever been in love, Emily?"

Em sighed and shook her head. "This is just between us, right?"

"Of course. I would never share anything that you and I have discussed."

She stared at Harley. Humiliating as it was, her managing editor should know the story. "I thought I was in love once because my father told me I should be. My fiancé checked all of good old Dad's boxes. Then I found out my father offered him a substantial dowry to propose. I realized too late that he was in love with my father's world, not me."

"Oh, my goodness, Emily. I am so sorry."

Em shrugged. "Don't be. I'm only glad I found out before the wedding."

"How long ago was this?"

"Five years." It was also the last time she'd seen her father.

"Maybe it's time to get back on the horse," Harley said.

"Yes, I'll do that. In my spare time." Em laughed as her gaze went to her long to-do list on the dry-erase board behind her.

Then she eyed the note she'd written after her interview with Buster Rutherford. *Check into the sheriff's background.* That investigation had gone nowhere, and Buster's cryptic remark continued to haunt her.

Her gaze went to the next note. *Soul Sisters.*

"Harley, what do you know about the Soul Sisters?" Em underlined that note with a marker. "I'm attending their meeting next Thursday."

Harley waved a palm. "As little as possible. Those ladies scare me."

"Really?" Em turned to look at Harley. "You're the second person to tell me something like that. I don't get it. These are church ladies. Isn't your mother part of the group?"

"Oh, no. My father is widowed."

Em sucked in a breath. "I'm so sorry, Harley. I didn't realize."

"I was really young. I don't even remember my mother. My

aunt pretty much raised me. She lives in Denver now." Harley slipped into the chair next to Em. "Tell you what, how about if I make my caramel brownies and you can bring them to the meeting?"

"Thank you. That would be wonderful, since I haven't unpacked much of my kitchen."

"No problem. I love to cook, thanks to my aunt."

"I can thank a very wise French nanny for my cooking abilities."

"Nanny?"

"Yes. I didn't exactly have a normal childhood," Emily admitted without emotion. She bore no bitterness about the declaration. Long ago, she had relegated her privileged yet lonely childhood to the "it is what it is" category.

"I'm starting to see that." Harley paused. "But how not normal?"

"I spent my formative years at boarding school and my summers with a nanny. My father doesn't like children underfoot."

"What about your mother?" Harley's expressive eyes revealed her horror and concern.

"She passed when I was young. No paternal relatives, and my father was estranged from my maternal grandmother. Apparently, she wanted joint custody and my father wouldn't hear of it, leading to legal action on his part."

Dismayed, Harley put a hand to her chest. "Could he do that?"

"Money and power. Enough of both, and you can do anything. The rules are different when you're rich." She shrugged. "I've had a parade of stepmothers all my life. As soon as I finished college and my father's reach couldn't yank me back, I began to search for my grandmother. It took a while, but thanks to a private detective, I was able to locate her."

"That's wonderful."

Em nodded. "It is." Her grandmother had provided something she sorely needed in her life: roots, consistency and tradition. "I spent all my holidays and vacations with her from that time on. Unfortunately, she passed recently. That's what took me so long to get to Aspen Creek."

"Oh, Emily. That's awful."

"At least we had time together." She swallowed, determined not to get all choked up. "Gram promised me she'd be waiting for me at the entrance to the pearly gates."

"What a lovely thought," Harley murmured. She glanced around the conference room, her gaze landing on the plant arrangement. "Is that new?"

"It arrived last week. Delivered by Lucy from the flower shop."

"Yes, but who sent such a lovely arrangement?"

It *was* a lovely arrangement, made up of dracaena, variegated ivy, green spathiphyllum and a few more plants she didn't recognize. "The sheriff's department sent it."

Harley offered a sly smile. "Chase Everett sent this?"

"No. I said the sheriff's department."

"And I said Chase Everett. Wow, the plot thickens. He gives you advice and sends you plants. Looks like you have his stamp of approval, Emily."

"Or he's saying 'welcome to town.' You might be reading too much into this." Em chuckled. She could only imagine how Harley might misconstrue things if she found out that Em was going to dinner at Chase's house on Sunday. For now, she'd keep that bit of information to herself. Things were changing between herself and the sheriff, and she was hesitant to hope that they could put their differences aside and become friends.

Em couldn't ignore the underlying attraction that flared between them, though she knew she ought to. There was no time for anything but the paper right now.

The beeping sound of a vehicle backing up had the managing editor jumping up to peer out the front window of the *Journal* once again.

"Here comes Bob Jones," she said as the white van parked in front of the office.

"The furnace," Em replied. "I pray he has good news."

Bob strolled through the front door wearing his perpetual smile, along with faded blue jeans, a fishing hat and a T-shirt with his fix-it shop's logo. "What's up, ladies?"

"All is well in the kingdom," Em replied, meeting him in the reception area.

He glanced around. "Where's my buddy, Byron?"

"Snoring in his bed, in the corner of the supply room," Em said. "I took him on a long walk this morning."

"That's what a big fella like Byron needs. Lots of exercise." Bob nodded and pulled off his hat, clutching it to his chest. "I have furnace news." The words were solemn and had Em tensing with nervousness. This could break her budget completely.

"Okay," she said slowly.

"I located that part we needed."

"Great." She waited for the inevitable *but.*

"Not so great. It'll be cheaper and faster to replace the furnace. Besides, this is autumn in Colorado. The first flake could happen at any time. In fact, it's late." He looked at Harley and then back to Emily. "Is the *Journal* still holding the annual First Flake Contest? Didn't see it in last week's issue. Everyone I know enjoys that contest, and the gift certificate to Sunshine Diner that goes to the winner is a sweet reward. Last year, my friend Patti Jo won and bought me lunch."

"You read the *Journal*?" Em asked. "But you're from Paradise."

"I read all the local papers. Most folks do. Four Forks, Paradise and Aspen Creek. We're one big happy family."

"I didn't realize," Em said.

"Yep. Your inauguration issue was terrific, Emily. I especially enjoyed the advice column."

"Thank you." Em beamed. "I'll pass that along to our columnist."

"You aren't going to tell me who it is?"

Em cocked her head and wagged a finger. "Now, Bob, that's a secret, but we'll schedule the First Flake Contest immediately." She nodded to Harley.

"I'm on it, boss," Harley said.

"So, Bob, how much will it cost to replace the furnace?"

He handed her the invoice. "I gave you a discount on labor."

"Thank you." Em's heart picked up speed, and her stomach became queasy as she read the totals and mentally balanced her checkbook. "That's a lot of zeros. But I can't continue like this much longer. I'm freezing up there, and that space heater isn't going to handle winter."

"Are you giving me the go-ahead then?"

She swallowed. "Yes. I guess I am."

"I'll put a rush on the order," Bob said. He slapped his cap back on his balding head and backed out of the office.

When her cell phone rang, Emily dug in her bag, praying it wasn't her father again. She hadn't heard from him since last Saturday. That was almost as troubling as his constant calls. When Douglas Baker wanted something, he didn't give up. He wanted her back in the fold and would not take no for an answer.

Her mistake had been calling her father when her grandmother died, thinking he might care. He cared about pulling Em back into his sphere of influence. That was as far as Douglas Baker's concern reached.

She pulled the phone out and flipped it over. The number was a welcome one—her real estate agent. She punched the green button with the pad of her finger and stepped into the conference room.

"Emily, this is Renata. We have a buyer for your condo."

"Wonderful." Relief washed over her. "For the full asking price?"

There was silence on the line for a moment. "Not exactly."

"How much, not exactly?" Emily asked.

"About five thousand under your lowball."

Emily groaned. That left enough feathers to barely cover the bottom of her nest once the bank and the outstanding bills at the *Journal* were paid.

"What do you want to do?" Renata asked.

"What *can* I do? The fact that they've been doing that road construction in front of my building for the last twelve months has not helped the situation." She shook her head. "Counter to see if they'll budge, but don't make it a deal breaker. I want that offer."

"Will do." Renata paused. "Cheer up. Since the condo is empty, we can expedite this and close in less than thirty days."

"Hallelujah to that."

"Do you want to start looking at property in Aspen Creek?"

"No. I'm living above the *Journal*. I'll stay put for now. The apartment is tiny, but it has a small yard that backs the alley for my dog. Besides, I own the building, and my bank account will be happy to hear that I won't be adding a second mortgage to my fiscal bottom line."

"You have a dog?"

Em smiled. "I do. No one has claimed him, so Byron is officially mine."

"It sounds like you're settling in. I'm glad, Emily. Sometimes things work out the way they're supposed to."

"Yes," Em murmured. "I guess they do."

"I'll counteroffer and send over the documents on the condo right away."

"Thank you."

"Oh, and Emily? I had an interesting call. A man looking for you on behalf of Douglas Baker."

"Oh?" Em lowered her voice.

"You don't think they meant *the* Douglas Baker, do you? That celebrity attorney. The one that's always on late-night news giving commentary on newsworthy legal stuff."

Em's stomach nose-dived. "What did you tell him?"

"Nothing. But he was quite persistent, which concerned me. Is there anything you want to talk about?"

"No, I'm sure it was a mistake."

"I hope so. Anyhow, I took his information. I'll send it to you in the email."

"Thanks, Renata." Em ended the call and stood staring at the phone for moments. Then she glanced at the clock and sighed. It was time to meet Sarah and Hope at the dog park. A daily bright spot. They'd developed a routine since Monday. Sarah now walked around the park with Em and Byron while Hope sat on the bench reading. She didn't say much, but chitchat wasn't necessary. Sometimes silence said more.

"Everything all right?" Harley asked from the doorway.

"It has to be," Em replied. "Because I don't have time for a meltdown."

"They're here!" Sarah called. The screen door slapped against the frame with a bang as she shot outside, her dark braids flying.

Chase followed behind, stunned at his niece's outburst. She sounded just like Phoebe. His chest tightened, reminding him of the narrow line between joy and grief.

"So they are," he murmured.

Emily moved up the brick path toward them carrying a cheerful bouquet of mixed flowers in one hand and Byron's leash in the other. She wore dark slacks and a pretty peach sweater that made her glow.

She smiled, and his heart thudded. Chase quickly looked

away while trying to figure out how one smile could knock him off-kilter.

Get it together, pal, he reminded himself.

Sarah stood on the porch, her hands clasped together tightly, excitement skittering across her face. "Byron. Come on, boy. Come on."

Chase stared with bemusement. He'd never seen Sarah so animated. After nearly a year of near silence, today marked a milestone. His heart swelled with joy, knowing he'd done right by his sister. It didn't escape him that Emily Taylor and her dog were responsible.

When Emily and Byron reached the front steps leading to his wraparound porch, the dog stopped, assessed the steps and plopped down, defeated.

Emily gave a short tug on the leash and sighed.

"So this is Byron," he said. Chase eyed the dog, confused.

"Yes," Emily said with another sigh. She held out the flowers to Chase. "Would you hold these for me, please? They're for Hope."

"What's for Hope?" His mother appeared behind him on the porch, smiling.

He handed her the flowers, his eyes on Emily, who bent down and scooped up the pup in her arms.

"Oh, they're beautiful," Hope said. "Thank you, Emily." Then she frowned. "Isn't he heavy?"

"Not bad yet," Emily replied as she started up the steps. "He's afraid of stairs. Going up and going down."

"Is he food motivated?" Chase asked as she set him on the porch. The dog shook himself, wagged his tail and raced in a circle, thrilled. "Because that dog isn't going to stay that size much longer."

"Correct. But no, Byron is not food motivated. I tried treats and an assortment of canine delicacies," she said.

"Wait a minute," he said. "You carry him up and down the

steps to your apartment?" Chase's eyes rounded as he recalled those steps.

"Uh-huh." Emily brushed the dog hair off her slacks. She glanced around the porch, her gaze taking in the wicker chairs with decorative pillows, the cranberry-colored porch swing and the striped jute rug. "Thank you so much for the invitation. This is lovely."

Chase raised his brows and looked at his mother. "Thanks. My mother hired a decorator when I wasn't looking. I don't dare invite her to my fishing cabin."

Hope chuckled.

"Come inside, Emily. Chase will show you around." Hope smiled. "Sarah, let's take Byron to the back and see if he approves of our yard."

"May I hold the leash?" Sarah asked eagerly.

Em handed the leash over.

Chase held the screen door as everyone moved inside. It occurred to him that this was the first time he'd had a woman who wasn't a family member or his mother's friend in his home. A journalist, no less. He prayed today was off the record.

"I'm never inviting you to my place," Emily murmured.

"Excuse me?" Chase replied.

"This is like a magazine layout. All those monochromatic shades of tan and slate and olive green. It's beautiful." She ran a hand over the soft gray throw draped over the back of the couch.

"Too much?" Chase grimaced. He'd given his mother free rein because it made her happy. Maybe it was a mistake.

"Not at all. It's comfortable, practical and very soothing. I'm sure it's wonderful to escape the world and come home to this." She turned around and nearly ran into him.

For a split second they stared at each other.

Emily swayed backward.

"Careful." Chase put a hand on her arm and instantly regretted the move. Touching Emily was not wise.

"Sorry," she said, her face turning pink. "I didn't realize you were that close."

Yep, he was close. Close enough to smell a hint of lemon perfume.

Chase nodded. "So you like my house?" He nearly did a face-palm. Maybe he could say something else dumb next.

"I do," she murmured.

"Wait until you see what she did with the kitchen. Come on."

He stepped into the space, and Emily followed.

"It smells amazing in here."

"Pot roast. My mother's secret recipe. However, I want to be clear—I *can* cook."

Emily's lips twitched. "I never doubted it for a minute."

She walked around, examining everything. Modern farm-house decor, his mother called it. Greige-stained kitchen cabinets and pale gray granite countertops. Whatever. The room was bright and cheerful, and the view through the sunroom and into the backyard never failed to make him smile and appreciate what he had here in Aspen Creek.

"That oven," Emily said. She studied the stainless steel appliance. "I'm in awe. A person could make a lot of chocolate chip cookies in that oven."

"Yeah, she got carried away in here, but hey, if I don't get reelected, I can sell the place to a tourist as a winter home and call it a day."

"Don't say that," Emily replied. "I keep my ear to the ground. You're going to be reelected."

Chase crossed his arms. "Nothing is a given, Emily. I'm working on my plan B. You're a savvy businesswoman. You probably are as well."

"I'm not there yet," she admitted. "Sure, I might have to lay off the delivery guy and cut back on staff hours, but I intend to remain ridiculously optimistic as long as possible."

Laughter spilled into the room through the screen door to the yard where Sarah raced around with Byron at her heels.

It was Sarah. Sarah was laughing. Chase hadn't heard the sound in so long that he stared, unable to speak. His throat tightened as he and Emily moved to the door to watch the two play.

"Have you decided what kind of dog you want?" Emily asked.

"I may have to rethink things." He shook his head. "Thank you for bringing Byron over."

"I'm being upstaged by a dog." She smiled. "Well worth it, to hear Sarah laughing."

Chase turned to look at her and found himself drowning in her brown eyes. It was like twelve years ago all over again. Chase was drawn to Emily as though they had some sort of invisible bond, which he knew was ridiculous.

A buzzer sounded on the oven and he blinked.

"Oh, those are my rolls," Hope called. "Chase, can you take them out while Sarah and I wash up?"

"I can do that," he called back.

Hope and Sarah came in from the yard, and Sarah moved past them to the sink. His niece wore a secret smile that said she was happy.

"Didn't you offer Emily something to drink?" Hope asked. "She's going to think we're terrible hosts."

"We were talking," Emily said. "No worries."

His mother dried her hands and looked from Emily to him. She raised her brow, a gesture Emily no doubt missed. But he knew his mother and was well aware of what was going on inside her matchmaking mind. "Talking is good," she finally said.

"Okay to be seated, Mom?" Chase asked.

"Of course." She smiled.

"Grandma, may I sit in your seat so I can watch Byron?" Sarah asked.

"That would be perfect. Emily, do you mind sitting between me and Chase?"

"Sure."

Chase shook his head. Now he'd have to hold Emily's hand during grace. His mother was clever. Very clever.

Once the meal began, his mother handed Emily a basket of rolls. "You're still attending the next Sisters' meeting, dear?"

"Yes. Absolutely."

"I'll save you a seat, then." She passed the butter.

"That's so nice of you."

"I wouldn't dream of letting you go alone. It's a fun group, but I am aware they can be a bit overwhelming."

"A bit?" Chase rolled his eyes. "They're like Darth Vader in skirts."

"Oh, you're exaggerating," Hope said.

Sarah giggled and they all looked at his niece. Her focus was out the door and on Byron, who had pressed his nose against the glass.

Chase couldn't help but laugh.

"Does Byron eat people food?" Sarah asked Emily.

"There are a few people foods that dogs can eat, but Byron has a special dog food that I bought at the vet's."

Sarah nodded. She quietly finished her meal and looked up at Chase. "Can I play with Byron now?"

There was no point keeping her at the table when all she wanted was to be with the dog. "Sure, stay in the sunroom for now," Chase said. "We can throw sticks with Byron after everyone finishes dinner."

She nodded, her face lighting up.

Emily's eyes were on Sarah as his niece slipped out of the room. Then she met his gaze, hers clearly noting again that Sarah needed a dog.

Chase smiled and focused on his meal.

"About that column in the paper, Emily," Hope interjected.

"It's simply brilliant. You should hear the gals at the Beauty Emporium. Everyone's trying to guess who wrote the letter and who your columnist is."

"That's great. It will sell papers." Emily wiped her mouth. "Where's the Beauty Emporium?"

Chase chuckled to himself. *Nice dodge, Emily.* Was it only obvious to him that she was the columnist and the author of the first letter?

"It's in the building with the Fashion Boutique. Next door," Hope replied. "We love the Emporium."

"We?" Chase noted. "Mom, you're starting to sound like you might stick around Aspen Creek."

"Maybe. I've been here enough since you took office to feel like a local." She looked at him. "I'm going to take that cruise with my girlfriends after the first of the year, then we can discuss the future."

"Sounds good to me." He'd learned the value of family long ago.

"However, if I do decide to take up permanent residence, I'll get my own place."

"There's plenty of room here, Mom."

"Dear, the presence of a law enforcement officer is a little stifling to my mah-jongg group."

"Those wild mah-jongg girls." Chase laughed. They did like to gossip, and when he entered the room, each one of them clammed up and turned red. He didn't want to know what they were talking about. Ever.

Chase's gaze met Emily's, and he smiled. "Sorry, we shouldn't be talking family business when we have a guest."

Em shook her head. "On the contrary. I'm enjoying myself."

"More roast, Emily?" Hope asked.

"No, thank you," she said. "I have to tell you, I haven't had a roast so tender and tasty in ages."

"Oh, you're so sweet. Thank you." She stood. "Chase, why

don't you clear the dishes and I'll go get that icebox cake from the garage refrigerator."

"Let me help," Emily said when his mother left the room.

"Seriously? Do you want me to get grounded for letting a guest help with the dishes?" He stacked the plates and carried them to the sink. Emily stood and looked out into the sunroom. Silence stretched for a minute before she turned to him. "You know, I thought this was going to be awkward."

He turned off the water and looked at her. "Yeah, me, too."

"It's been fun. I like your family," she murmured.

"Does that include me?" Chase teased.

"It does. You're not so bad once you let your guard down. You should do it more often."

"I'll give that some thought, too," he said. Lots of thought, because he knew that life was safe as long as he distanced himself from the world and kept the wall firmly in place. He wasn't sure what would happen if he let Emily in, and he was terrified to find out.

Chapter Seven

On Tuesday, Chase opened the door of the Aspen Creek sheriff's office to find Cora-Lee leaning back in her chair reading the *Journal*. The office admin released a snort of laughter and slapped her hand on the desk, tipping over her coffee cup.

"What's so funny?" he asked.

Cora-Lee jumped up and reached for the box of tissues. "The paper, Sheriff." She grinned as she mopped the stream of liquid that ran across the newspaper and dripped off the desk. "Boy, she sure told that guy a thing or two."

"She who? Told who what?"

"*Dispatches from the Heart.* Haven't you been following the column? Best thing in the *Journal* in years." She paused. "The article about you is pretty good, too. I had no idea you were such a scholar."

"A scholar?"

"Sure. Says right here you are. Hard to miss. It's on the front page alongside your picture. Was that taken at the lake? You look contemplative."

Contemplative. He probably resembled a deer caught in headlights. Front-page news. He'd managed to ride just under the radar for the last four years. Now here he was campaigning to save his job and his family. While a necessity, the whole public-eye thing continued to unnerve him.

"I'll have to take your word for it, since you're reading my paper." He cocked his head to examine the soggy newsprint.

"Am I?"

"Yeah, and I had high hopes to check the hardware store ads. Fishing equipment usually goes on sale at the end of September."

Cora-Lee waved several damp pages of newspaper in the air. "I'll be done in a minute."

"Ah, you keep it." Chase sniffed the air. "What kind of coffee is that?"

"You weren't supposed to be in until noon, so I made the chocolate biscotti blend."

"My meeting in Four Forks was canceled."

"Try the coffee. A little open-mindedness won't hurt. You might like it." She nodded toward the pot. "Almost as good as the vanilla bean."

Chase grimaced. "I'll pass on the open-mindedness today. We're having regular boring coffee at the campaign dinner on Saturday, right?"

"Yes, sir."

"What exactly are we raising funds for again?"

"The election is a little over six weeks from today. We're already behind on advertising. These last few weeks are mighty important."

And if this were a normal timeline, he'd have known that he was running opposed months ago. Buster might be a write-in candidate, but the man was campaigning like he had an endless campaign budget.

Chase took a deep breath. "I get that, Cora-Lee, but you haven't answered my question."

She reached for a clipboard on the wall and whipped out a piece of paper and handed it to him. "We'll blast the radio stations and put up a billboard or two. Not as many as Buster already has up, but it'll do. Then there's campaign buttons, pens, lip balm and bumper stickers. We also have to pay for a full-color ad in the *Journal*. Oh, and I reserved a booth at the Harvest Festival. It helped that the Soul Sisters are running the festival." She shook her head. "Unfortunately, my festival chair resigned and I'm going to have to find another. Quick."

"Excuse me?"

"Never mind. Not your problem."

"Glad to hear that." He eyed the paper in his hands. "But back to the booth at the Harvest Festival. Why do I need one?"

Cora-Lee released a snort of impatience. "So you can talk to voters and pass out the aforementioned campaign items." She paused. "They call that stuff swag."

"I'll take your word for it."

"By the way, I've come up with your campaign slogan." Cora-Lee grinned. "'Everett for Sheriff. Making the world a better place.'"

Chase cringed as she recited using air quotes. She forgot to mention a chicken in every pot.

"What do you think?"

"I'm running for sheriff. Not president."

"All right, then. I've got a backup slogan." She stared him right in the eyes, like a preacher with a fiery sermon about to be delivered. "'Integrity, honesty and experience. Everett for Sheriff.'"

"Fine. That'll do."

Cora-Lee grinned. "I need to go over the details for Saturday with you while we're at it."

"What details? We eat and I make a speech." Chase frowned. His head told him the details were part and parcel of running a campaign. But this was unknown territory for him, and he struggled with being overwhelmed and worried it wasn't going to keep him in the job he wanted and needed.

"Look, Sheriff, you're going to have to get a little more enthusiastic if this is going to work."

"Enthusiastic?" He rubbed his chin. "Did your husband have to campaign?"

"A time or two, when the mayor would bring in someone to run against him. The thing is, the mayor wants a yes-man. He was sorely disappointed that my husband was not that man. I imagine you've disappointed him as well. You earned that badge. I can manage your campaign, but the rest is up to you. Can you smile and shake hands for a few weeks or not?"

"You're right. I apologize." Chase looked at Cora-Lee. "I appreciate the sermon."

"No problem." Cora-Lee pulled out another paper and offered it to him. "Here's the agenda for the evening. What do you think?"

"Nick Saunders agreed to speak. That's great." Chase's eyes widened when he got to the last item on the list. "The Rio Grande County Cattle Queen will provide entertainment?"

"I can hardly believe it myself." Cora-Lee offered a pleased nod. "I know her grandmother or we'd never have booked her on such short notice. I had to promise a seat at the main table next to you. Plus, we had to add burger sliders to the menu."

"And what's her entertainment?"

"We have a choice. The woman is very versatile. She won the competition playing the piano, but she's also been featured yodeling at the Alamosa Rodeo."

The circus is coming to town. Chase tipped back his hat and massaged his forehead. He met the office admin's gaze. "I'll work on my enthusiasm, but promise me there will not be yodeling, Cora-Lee."

"Fine. Are you okay with the deejay?"

"I'll need to see a playlist." Chase turned on his heel. "I'll be back." He strode out the way he came, crossing the street to the diner, where the coffee could be relied upon to be strong and black without unnecessary flavors.

"Help you, Sheriff?" Amy asked from behind the counter.

"An extra-large black coffee to go, please. And I need to get a copy of the *Journal*."

"Paper sold out within an hour of Harley dropping them off this morning, but I'll be right back with your coffee."

Chase glanced around the diner, where everyone seemed to be face-first in the *Journal*. Well, didn't that just figure? When he glimpsed his own photo on the front, he could only shake his head. As suspected, he looked ridiculous.

He couldn't believe she'd used that photo. The woman should have gone into politics—she sure knew how to finesse a situation. Chase nearly laughed aloud recalling her popping out of the bushes at the lake.

"Here you go, Sheriff."

Chase dropped some bills on the glass counter and grabbed the lidded paper coffee cup. "Next week, could you set aside a copy of the *Journal* for me?"

"Oh, absolutely. I'll do that." She grinned. "Nice picture of you."

He only grumbled in response. Outside, Liam Olson, proprietor of the barbershop next door to the diner, sat on a bench squinting as he read the *Journal*. He held the paper inches from his nose while his reading glasses sat on top of his bald head.

"Hey there, Liam."

"Chase."

"Why don't you put your glasses on?"

"Can't find 'em."

"On your head."

"Well, what do you know." Liam laughed and slid the glasses into place.

Chase chuckled.

"Nice write-up about you in today's edition," Liam said. "I didn't know you graduated summa cum laude from the University of Denver."

Chase glanced at the paper. So Emily had done her homework, just like he knew she would. What else had she dug up?

"That's in there?" he asked.

"Sure is. Haven't you read the paper yet?"

He pushed back the brim of his hat. "Can't seem to find a copy."

"I bet they're flying off the counter in the diner faster than the muffins. That Emily Taylor knows how to stir things up."

That much, Chase knew, was true. "Do you have any extra at the barbershop?" he asked.

"No, but the hardware store keeps a bunch. Murphy Sr. puts a few away under the counter. Told me so himself."

"I'll check it out. Thanks, Liam."

The barber waved a palm. "See you Saturday at your campaign dinner."

"I'm afraid so," Chase mumbled. He walked half a block to Murphy's Hardware with coffee in his hand and pushed open the door.

Ryan Murphy greeted him with a welcome smile. "Hey there, Mr. Candidate. Saw your mug on the front page of the *Journal*. How's it feel to be a celebrity?"

Chase glared.

"Okay, then." Murph chuckled. "I guess you're here to look at those reels we have on sale. Best price all year."

"Yeah. I mean, no." Chase paused. "Do you have an extra copy of the *Journal*?"

"Let me see if we have any left." Murph searched around the cash register, lifting items out of the way. "Did you read that advice column?"

"Haven't read anything yet." Chase shook his head. "Liam says to look under the counter. He claims your father stashes a few there."

Murph ducked down to examine the shelves and popped up

with a paper in his hand. "Liam was right. Now, let me show you those reels."

"You mind if I come back later?"

"Sure. No problem." He paused. "I hear you and Emily Taylor were fishing."

"Who told you that?"

"I dunno. One of the guys at the fire station."

"We were not fishing. She's a journalist and I'm running for office. That would be a conflict of interest."

"You have to wait until after the election to date her?" Murph eyed him and shook his head. "That might be too late."

"I'm not interested in Emily Taylor."

"Huh. That's not what I heard." Murph clucked his tongue. "You know, Chase. Time passes when we aren't looking. You wait too long and you'll find yourself alone with your dog. Except you don't even have a dog."

"Says the man who doesn't see what's right under his nose."

"What are you talking about?" Murph asked.

"I'm talking about Harley Augustine."

The words had Murph frowning. "What does Harley have to do with this? She's my best buddy."

"Murph, Harley is a woman. She is not your best buddy. Open your eyes before you find yourself alone with *your* dog."

"Wait a minute. Are you insulting Henry? He may be a mutt, but Henry graduated top of his class at obedience school."

Chase rolled his eyes. "No. I'm insulting you." Tucking the paper under his arm, he strode back to his office. Obviously, Murph hadn't figured out that one of the letters in Emily's advice column was about him.

When he pulled open the door to the sheriff's office, Cora-Lee was waiting for him. She still had the clipboard in her hands.

"Sheriff—"

"Hold my calls." He quickly walked into his office and closed the door before she could get another word in.

There was satisfaction in slowly peeling off the lid of the cup and inhaling the strong scent of uncompromised beans. Coffee, the way God intended. He sipped. Perfect. Exactly what he needed. Carefully unfolding the paper, he sat down and leaned back in his chair.

The picture of himself smack-dab in the middle of the front page seemed unnecessarily large. Ignoring it, he moved to page five and *Dispatches from the Heart*.

Dear Honest Man,
Clearly, you are confused.

Chase grinned as he read the rest of the letter that explained the columnist's difference of opinion about men's and women's approaches to romance. The whole thing reeked of Emily's brand of sass and intellectual wit. He would have to give this some thought before he answered. The key would be to keep the repartee going without revealing himself as the author of the letters.

Much as he disliked the front-page coverage, he turned back to read the article that accompanied his photo. Yeah, Emily had done her work, all right. How had she found out that he worked on the college newspaper? There were other details that told him the editor of the *Journal* knew how to information-gather.

Sure, he was a public official, and a political candidate. Scrutiny came with the territory. Yet, he found himself unsettled.

What would happen if she realized his trail ended at college? There would be no record of Chase Everett before that, because he'd changed his name after he was acquitted.

It was only a matter of time. When, not if.

Was this the end of the story? Or in the ensuing weeks until the election, would Emily continue to dig into his past until they both regretted her journalistic skill? Emily had the know-how to destroy everything he'd worked for.

Em reached for the container next to her on the car seat. Even after further pleading, Harley could not be persuaded to attend the Soul Sisters meeting. Thankfully, she'd kept her word and sent along her brownies. Her amazing brownies. The aromas of caramel and chocolate filled the vehicle, and Emily barely resisted the urge to stay in the Volkswagen and eat them all instead of heading to Cora-Lee's door.

She gave herself a little pep talk. *Hope will be there. You'll have one friendly face.*

The afternoon had brought a late rain, which curtailed her trip to the dog park with Byron. The Labernese had whined on and off for an hour when the clock approached his usual park visit. She'd tried to get him to go out in the rain for a walk around the block, but he declined. The dog had strong opinions.

An hour ago, the precipitation had stopped and the skies cleared. Only a rainbow, spread against the pale blue sky, remained. Surely that was a sign of good things to come.

She stared out at the wet landscape through her open window. A slight wind shivered the trees, causing a tiny rainfall. The scents of grass and clean air whispered past. There was something cleansing about rain, reminding her of fresh starts.

And wasn't that really why she was in Aspen Creek? For a fresh start at her new life. To prove she could have a forever future without her father's money.

That meant being brave. Surely she wasn't afraid of a group of church ladies. After all, she'd held her own against Douglas Baker, hadn't she? Not many people could say that. Yet she had.

Which served to remind her that she hadn't heard from her father in a week. Perhaps he'd given up.

Buoyed by that thought, she stepped out of the car and walked past the bumper-to-bumper vehicles that ran nearly an entire block approaching Cora-Lee's one-story white colonial home framed with climbing ivy. In the front of the house, pots overflowed with begonias welcoming guests. Though it was now mid-September, they still held their scarlet bloom. Along the side of the house, a riot of multicolored petunias danced in the slight breeze.

Em stood on the stoop for a few moments, gathering courage and wondering how the women in all those cars lining the street would fit inside the little house in front of her. She raised her hand and gave a hesitant knock. The front door burst open, and she had her answer: The house was packed with women, the noise level slightly below a roar.

"Welcome to the Soul Sisters." A tiny woman, whose white hair held a tint of purple, offered a broad smile. Behind her cat-eye glasses, bright blue eyes sparkled. Her name tag, stuck to the lapel of a lavender blazer, said, "Hello. My name is Minnie."

"Hi. I'm Emily Taylor from the *Journal*."

"Cora-Lee," Minnie hollered over her shoulder. "It's the newspaper lady."

"Don't leave her out on the stoop. Invite her in," Cora-Lee called back.

Minnie laughed. "Silly me. Come on in, Edna."

"Emily. It's Emily."

"I'll be the one taking your membership fee," Minnie continued. "We take cash or card."

"Okay. I'll be sure to take care of that this evening."

"Now would be good."

Em's eyes rounded. Minnie certainly was assertive. Well, good for her. "How much did you say?"

"Fifty dollars."

"Fifty dollars. Isn't that a little steep?"

"We're a very active charitable organization. That takes cold, hard cash."

"I see. Could you hold this?" Em handed her the container of brownies.

"Sure. What is in it?"

"Brownies." Em dug in her purse and pulled out several crinkled bills. There would be no lattes from the diner this week.

"I make cream puffs," Minnie said. "Everyone loves my cream puffs. They're famous. Be sure to try one."

"I will," Em said. She counted the bills and offered them to Minnie. "Here you go."

"She joined," Minnie yelled as she handed back the brownies.

"No need to shout, Minnie. I'm right here." Cora-Lee appeared and turned to Emily. "Chase said to expect you. Right on time, too. What did you bring?"

"Brownies," Emily murmured, handing over the container once again.

"How nice." Cora-Lee gave the brownies to Minnie, who remained at her side like a dutiful soldier. "Would you put these on the buffet table, please?"

Minnie nodded crisply and turned away to complete her mission.

Cora-Lee took Emily by the arm. "So glad you could make it. Now, don't let me forget that you and I need to schedule an appointment to discuss the *Journal*'s coverage of the election. I'd like to see a few stories featuring Sheriff Everett in the paper. Not the usual stuff. I'm thinking something showing his softer side."

Em perked up at the words. Softer side? Well, who would know better than Cora-Lee? "Do you think he'll agree?"

"I'm handling his campaign. You're going to have his complete cooperation from now on." Cora-Lee leaned closer. "We won't discuss it tonight. He's here."

"What?" Em's eyes popped wide at the comment. She glanced around. "Chase is here?"

"Yes. His niece as well."

"I thought this group was women only." And she distinctly recalled his warning about attending. Why would Chase come to a meeting of a group that he considered "Darth Vader in skirts"?

"I have no clue why he's here, but it's gotten some of our younger members all atwitter. They like the tall, dark and handsome type. Go figure." She nodded toward the interior of the house. "Come on in. Find a seat. If you'll excuse me, I've got to get this party started."

Cora-Lee moved to a podium set up in the living room and banged a gavel. Em jumped. Around her, the room fell silent. At least two dozen women sat on folding chairs scattered throughout a large space. Additional chairs spilled into a connected dining room. Even those standing froze, all eyes on Cora-Lee.

"Before the meeting begins, I'd like to introduce our guests of honor today," Cora-Lee said. "First, the new editor and publisher of the *Aspen Creek Journal*, Emily Taylor. She is now a card-carrying Soul Sister. Paid her dues and everything."

A light round of applause and the buzz of voices followed the introduction. Em offered a hesitant smile in return. Her gaze spanned the room, where she saw a few familiar and smiling faces: Lucy Reynolds from the flower shop, Vesta from the veterinary clinic and Sloane Flanagan, the tea merchant, who was Cora-Lee's niece. But no Hope.

"I will trust you to introduce yourselves to Ms. Taylor. Additionally, Sheriff Everett and his niece, Sarah, are here to observe the meeting." Cora-Lee looked around, then smiled. "Aha, there they are by the exit."

Em followed the curious glances of the women to the dining room, where Chase and Sarah sat near a patio door. Of course, law enforcement officers preferred to sit by an exit with their eye on the room. Sarah sat next to Chase, leaning against her uncle and holding his arm tightly, as though she wanted to hide.

She could well relate to the little girl's feeling.

The gavel banged again. "We'll come to order in approximately forty minutes," Cora-Lee said. "Let me remind you that we are on a tight schedule this evening. All right, then. Minnie, will you lead us in prayer?"

Minnie stood and bowed her head. "Please bless this food, Lord. Let's eat."

Like the starting gun at a race, everyone moved toward the buffet table. Em wove her way through the room, trying to reach Chase. Now she knew how salmon swimming upstream felt. When Em reached the dining room, she found herself behind a line of women eager to eat. Ducking around them, she finally made it to Chase and Sarah. She dropped into an empty chair next to the little girl.

"What are you two doing here? Where's Hope?" Em asked.

"We're your moral support." Chase looked at his niece. "Right, Sarah?"

"Yes." She sighed. "Did you bring Byron?"

"No, I'm sorry. He's at home."

Sarah sighed again.

Em met Chase's gaze. "Seriously, why are you here?"

She looked him up and down. He wasn't even in uniform. And now she understood why the women around the room were sneaking glances at him. She didn't blame them. Chase was quite formidable in Levi's and a black T-shirt. *Tall, dark and handsome* was no exaggeration. And with impressive biceps. She focused on the wallpaper behind him.

"I told you," he said. "Moral support. My mother had to drive to Denver. She has a friend who needs her. It was unexpected." He cocked his head toward his niece, indicating he didn't want to discuss it in front of Sarah.

"Moral support?"

"That's right."

Em's heart got all squishy at the words. Chase Everett was here to support her.

"Thank you," she said softly.

He nodded and eyed the buffet table. "You better get in line. They expect you to try everything."

"They do?"

"Yeah, my mother told me to tell you that. They get insulted if you don't."

"What about you?" She glanced over at the line to the buffet table again. Thankfully, it had dwindled.

"We ate before we got here." Chase turned to his niece. "Pancakes for dinner. Sarah's favorite."

"Oh, I'm sorry I missed that."

"Maybe next time you can come over," Sarah said. "Uncle Chase makes good pancakes."

"Oh, yes, please." Em stood, prepared to get in line. "Okay, then. I'll do my best."

"Emily?"

"Yes?" She turned toward him. Gaze intent, he motioned for her to come closer. A shiver passed over her as she leaned near.

"Stay away from the cream puffs."

"What? Why?" She frowned. "You're joking, right?"

"It's a matter of life and death. I'll explain later. Trust me on this."

"Okay, then. No cream puffs."

Em assessed the table and nearly groaned. If she had known how much food she would be required to sample, she would have fasted for a week. She made her way around the table, taking minuscule servings of Swedish meatballs, gelatin pretzel salad, lasagna with garlic bread, mystery casserole and miniature wieners in barbecue sauce. On the other end of the table, ambrosia salad, pistachio Bundt cake, zucchini bread and assorted pies beckoned. She noted the untouched cream puffs and the near-empty container of Harley's brownies.

Assessing her plate, Em checked her watch. Less than thirty minutes to eat everything, or risk offending two dozen women. The seat next to Sarah was now occupied, so Em found one near the front of the room.

At first, she dug in with determined enthusiasm, but with every other bite, she was approached by a member of the group introducing herself and welcoming her to Aspen Creek, which required Em to ignore the food in an effort to chat with each woman and encourage them to submit story leads to the *Journal*.

Representatives of several area churches greeted her with invitations to visit their Sunday services. That would be quite a few Sundays. Em took the cards and brochures and tucked them in her purse to peruse later. This was good. She'd like to find a nice church to call home.

"Ready for dessert, Edna?" Minnie asked, pausing at Em's chair.

Em looked at the tiny purple-haired woman and decided to pick her battles. Edna. Emily. What did it matter? Instead, she smiled. "I'm still savoring this wonderful meal."

Her only hope was to keep nibbling as the meeting began and hope they were distracted enough not to notice. Fortunately, she snagged a large paper napkin to assist in a potential cover-up.

"Don't forget my cream puffs." Minnie smiled. "I'll be sure to set aside a few for you."

"No, that won't be—"

Cora-Lee pounding the wooden gavel interrupted their conversation. The group fell silent. Someone stood and began to read the minutes of the last meeting. The speaker's voice was drowned out by the woman seated next to Em.

"And then I had that abdominal surgery," the woman told her friend. "I had him do a tummy tuck while he was at it."

As she took a sip of coffee, Emily heard her name called.

"I second the motion," Minnie yelled.

"All those in favor—"

Em jumped to her feet, jostling the cup and dripping coffee on her slacks. "Wait. Wait. I didn't hear the motion."

All eyes were upon her, and she knew her face would be splotchy and red from embarrassment.

"I nominated you as replacement chair for the Harvest Festival," Cora-Lee said with a satisfied smile.

"But, but—" Em protested.

"I'd like to co-chair the event," Chase called out from the back of the room.

"You aren't a member, Sheriff Everett," Cora-Lee stated. "And you don't look like a sister."

A wave of laughter rose. Em was not laughing.

"Make me a member, then," he replied firmly. "I'd like to help with the Harvest Festival."

Cora-Lee narrowed her gaze. For a moment, the two stared at each other in a silent battle of wills. Then the Soul Sisters' president turned to Minnie. "What do the bylaws say?"

Minnie flipped through a large notebook. "Doesn't say he can't."

"*Fine*, you're a member."

"Welcome," Minnie said. "That's fifty dollars, cash or card."

Em raised a hand. "Um, excuse me. What exactly does this position entail?"

"The committee runs itself," Cora-Lee replied. "Not to worry. The title is almost honorary. You'll have very little to do, and we have a handy-dandy binder with detailed instructions."

Not to worry? Em opened her mouth and then closed it again. Resistance was obviously futile, so she simply nodded and slunk back into her chair. Besides, she wanted to…*needed* to be accepted into the Aspen Creek fold for the paper to succeed, and this might be the only way to do so. And Chase was going to help her. What a turn of events this was.

Minnie appeared in front of her with a giant three-ring binder. "Here you go, Edna. It's all in here."

Em glanced at the tome and grimaced. What had she gotten herself into?

The next thirty minutes were a whirlwind of nominations and voting, nailing down positions for a laundry list of charitable events coming up. A list of events that could be featured in another new column for the *Journal*. Em took copious notes.

Cora-Lee was nothing short of impressive. The president managed to move through the next three months of assignments with amazing efficiency and speed. She fielded questions and delegated like a pro.

"Our last order of business is Sheriff Everett's reelection campaign," Cora-Lee continued. "I'll need ten volunteers to assist with that."

Dozens of hands shot up, and a thrum of excited whispers and giggles spread through the room. This was apparently the Sheriff Everett fan club.

"Order, please." Cora-Lee banged her gavel. "Minnie, get a list of those with their hands up. We'll contact you if you are chosen."

"Before we adjourn, I'd like you all to remember that the two-year term of the board president will end in December. We will be soliciting nominations for the positions of president, secretary and treasurer at the next meeting."

"Cora-Lee's been president for twenty years, you know," Minnie whispered.

"Is that legal?" Em asked.

"No one else wants the job."

Cora-Lee looked over at Em and offered a fond smile. "I imagine we can find something for you on the board as well."

Em slid lower in her seat, grateful when the gavel was pounded a final time.

"We are adjourned."

A moment later, Chase was at her side. He nodded toward

the door. "Come on, let's get out of here before Cora-Lee pulls another fast one."

"I should say my goodbyes."

"Nope. See that door? Aim for it." He took Sarah's hand. "You can blame me."

"How can I blame you? We didn't come together."

"Emily, you're killing me. Do you want to end up in charge of litter patrol on the highway for the next six months?"

"You're right." She scooped up her purse and the giant binder and headed for the door.

Once outside, where the sun had disappeared, making way for the evening, Em took a deep breath, feeling like she had masterminded a prison break.

Chase's phone rang. He pulled it out, and his face paled. "Everett here. Yeah, got it. I'll be right there."

"Everything okay?"

"No," he said with a glance at Sarah. "I hate to even ask, but I've got a situation, and I can't take Sarah."

"Say no more. I'm happy to stay with Sarah."

"Can we get Byron?" Sarah asked.

"Sure, honey," Em said.

Chase dug in his pocket and pulled out a ring of keys. He handed her a single key. "I'll be home as fast as I can."

Em put her hand on his arm. "Do what you have to do. Sarah and I will be fine."

He looked at her hand on his arm, his expression unreadable. "Thanks, Emily. I owe you one."

"No. We're even. You and Sarah were my moral support tonight. I appreciate it." She met his gaze and studied his face for a moment. Every time she thought she had Chase figured out, she didn't. "Besides," she continued. "You saved my life. I would have eaten a cream puff if you hadn't warned me."

A small smile touched his lips. "There is that." He turned to

Sarah. "I'll get your booster seat. You explain your nighttime routine to Emily, okay, kiddo?"

His niece nodded solemnly.

It took Sarah ten minutes to explain her very detailed routine. Em stared at Chase's niece, who sat in the back seat, buckled in with Byron buckled in next to her.

Sarah was a forty-year-old trapped in a seven-year-old's body. Yes, routine was important while she grieved, but there was much to be said for spontaneity. For simply being a kid.

"Bedtime is eight thirty?"

"Uh-huh."

Em glanced at her watch. They had an hour and a half. "Sweetie, we're driving to the ice cream shop in Four Forks. They have the best sprinkles anywhere and we can go through the drive-through and get a pup cup for Byron."

"What's a pup cup?"

"It's whipped cream in a little cup just for dogs. No sprinkles."

"But I can have sprinkles?"

"Yes, lots of sprinkles for you and me. And we'll be home in plenty of time for you to floss, brush and knock off most of your bedtime list. Okay with you?"

Sarah grinned so wide that Em could see she was missing a lower incisor. Em chuckled. This was progress.

The smile hadn't lessened an hour later, as they got back in the car to head home. A peek in the rearview mirror revealed that both Sarah and Byron had whipped cream on their faces as well.

"What did you think about those sprinkles?" she asked.

"The best," Sarah said. "I'll tell my mom about them when I pray tonight."

Em's breath caught at the words that hit so very close to home. She turned in her seat to look at Sarah. "Do you talk to your mom, Sarah?"

The little girl nodded shyly. "I told her about Byron and you."

"My momma is in heaven, too, and I talk to her sometimes." Em smiled, her heart aching.

"You do?"

"Yes," Em replied softly.

Sarah stared at Em for a moment. "Can we have sprinkles again?" she finally asked. "And bring Uncle Chase with us?"

"Yes," Em replied. She fastened her seat belt and started the car. "We absolutely can. I think Uncle Chase deserves sprinkles."

Lots of sprinkles. Chase Everett was a good man to take in his sister's child, and she had better be very careful, because the more she got to really understand the man, the closer she came to falling for him. And that was not on her to-do list.

Chapter Eight

Chase drove slowly down Main Street. The lights were still on in the *Journal* offices. He glanced at his watch. Eleven in the evening on a Friday and Emily was still working? Grace had often stayed late. But not this late.

He ought to check on things and thank Emily for staying with Sarah last night. They'd hardly had a chance to talk when he got home. It was late, and the call to Ennis and Dolly Towers's home outside Aspen Creek had left him emotionally exhausted. Emily and Byron left five minutes after he'd arrived.

All he could get out of Sarah was that they'd had the best sprinkles in the world, which had to be true, as he'd found sprinkles scattered all over her bedroom floor when he went to wake her up for school this morning.

Getting out of his patrol vehicle, he glanced up and down the street. Everything was quiet. Even the Sunshine Diner had stopped serving an hour ago and was dark. He put his hand on the doorknob of the *Journal* office. Not only was the door unlocked, but the entire knob wiggled as though it was about to fall apart.

"Hello?" He stepped into the main reception area. Byron padded straight to him. "I guess you're the watchdog, huh, pal?"

The animal knocked his head into Chase's knee and looked up at him hopefully.

"I can take a hint." He rubbed Byron's head and jowls and then peeked into the first doorway on his right.

Emily was there, sure enough. Sleeping. Her face was buried in her folded arms, which rested on an oval conference table.

A large plant arrangement sat in the middle of the table. Chase reached over and pulled out the card.

Welcome to Aspen Creek, from the Sheriff's Department.

Well done, Cora-Lee.

He glanced up at the dry-erase board where Emily had written in bold letters, "Candidate profiles." And farther down, "In-depth background information for October."

Chase frowned, tamping down annoyance. Emily was determined. He'd give her that. He was equally determined to block her digging.

She moved in her sleep, turning her head so her thick hair, brown with hints of red, flowed around her. He could see the long lashes resting on her face. Emily Taylor was a bundle of energy. Seeing her still was like witnessing a hummingbird pause.

What was her story? Something drove the woman. What it was, he couldn't be sure. A subtle shift had happened between them. He felt it, and he knew she had, too. Why did she have to be a journalist? A journalist who didn't realize she held the power to destroy the life he'd made for himself and his niece in Aspen Creek.

He cleared his throat, hoping to wake the hummingbird without startling her.

"Emily?" He called her name a little louder. "Emily."

"Hmm?" She raised her head and smiled softly at him. "Chase?"

The smile took his breath away.

Then she grimaced. "Oh, my neck. I'm going to pay for falling asleep at my desk." She stretched and yawned.

"You need to lock the door at night and when you're alone here."

"Didn't I?"

"No, and your watchdog isn't much help. He's poised to lick an intruder to death."

Emily chuckled. "Lock the door. I'll do that from now on, Sheriff. You aren't going to ticket me, are you?"

"We don't ticket for failure to use common sense."

"Oh, please. What are you so worried about anyway?" She rubbed her eyes. "We haven't printed anything that could annoy anyone as far as I can tell."

"You never know."

She studied him. "I think you're being paranoid, but I'll be sure to lock the doors if it makes you feel better."

Was he being paranoid after the domestic situation last night? Or were his growing feelings for Emily bringing out the desire to protect her? Either scenario was worrisome.

"Thank you." He glanced at the clock. "Kind of late, isn't it?"

"Yes. It's been a long day. The *Journal* goes to the printer on Fridays."

As they spoke, Byron came in, put a paw on Emily's lap, whined and padded out of the room.

"What's he doing?"

"He's telling me that he wants to be picked up and taken upstairs. It's past his bedtime."

"And now he's gone?" Chase stepped into the lobby and glanced around.

"He's in the supply room. I keep a bed in there during the day. It's warmer than out here."

He nodded. "You're right. It does feel a little chilly in here."

"The windows don't help, but I think I mentioned that the Beast is having problems."

"The Beast?"

"The furnace. You recommended Bob Jones from Paradise.

He's been here and ordered a new one. He'll install it next week." She sighed. "I'm hoping it will last until then. The good news is that the replacement is supposed to last for the next fifteen to twenty years."

"You plan to stick around that long?" Emily Taylor in Aspen Creek for the long haul. Why didn't he believe that? Maybe because she seemed destined for more than this town. Yet, the idea of having her here on a permanent basis had more appeal than he would have admitted to a few weeks ago.

"I'm starting to think I don't have a choice," Emily replied. "I've invested everything I own in this paper." She glanced at his uniform. "What are you doing out and about so late anyhow? Still on duty? Didn't I see you out patrolling early this morning?"

"You probably did."

"Is this normal for you?"

"I've got a deputy on vacation a couple of days this week and one out sick. I'm covering his shift tonight."

"Long day for you as well, then." Emily stood and stretched. "Bottled water?"

"I'm fine, thanks."

She walked to the back room, came back with two waters and handed him one. "Take it. I don't like to drink alone."

Chase smiled. "Thanks again for staying with Sarah."

Emily sat back down at the conference table and opened her water. "It really wasn't a big deal. Did she tell you we broke all the rules?"

"No. But there were signs. Sprinkles on the bedroom floor, the missing toothpaste cap. When I asked how it went last night, she giggled and said something about a pup cup."

"We had fun. Your girl is very obedient, you know."

"Yeah, that's what worries me." He and Phoebe had been a handful, as his mother liked to remind him. Sarah had always been serious, while Phoebe was notoriously laid-back. Since her mother's death, Sarah had become even more somber. A little adult.

"Don't overthink," Emily replied. "You're doing everything right. It'll get better."

"I hope so." He twisted open the cap on the water bottle and took a swallow.

"Is your mother back from Denver?"

"Not yet. I have a babysitter helping out. I don't know when Mom will be back. Her friend is going through a rough patch."

"I'm sorry to hear that. I'll be praying."

"Thank you."

"What was your law enforcement situation last night?" she asked.

"A domestic. That's all I can say." Domestic situations were the worst, though they were why he went into law enforcement. To prevent what nearly happened to his mother from happening to another woman. He knew only too well how one moment could change your life forever. It had changed his.

Being labeled a murderer during the months leading up to the trial had haunted him for years. No kid should be in that position. No family should.

"Isn't Colorado a mandatory-arrest state for domestic violence?"

"Yeah."

Last night's had been particularly challenging. Something had triggered Ennis, and he'd been arrested on a misdemeanor charge for menacing behavior. Chase had hauled him in. Unfortunately, his wife refused to leave the home. That concerned him more than anything.

"Sounds like a rough night all around."

"Yeah," he repeated.

Emily nodded. "And what about the cream puffs?"

Chase hadn't expected the question and smiled. "It's been an unspoken rule never to eat them for as long as I've lived here. She brings them to all the community events."

"I'm not sure I understand. What are you supposed to do with them?"

"That's an excellent question. I was advised to push them around on my plate so as not to offend Minnie."

"I appreciate the warning. Last night was challenging enough. Death by cream puff would have been humiliating."

"Did you have a chance to look at the Harvest Festival binder?" he asked, noting the large three-ring notebook on the table.

"Yes, and I did a little investigative work. It turns out Cora-Lee had a difference of opinion with the former festival chair. She only recently resigned. The good news is, Cora-Lee is correct. Most of the work is in progress. The former chair appointed four Soul Sisters to the festival. All we have to do is follow up with them. As far as I can tell, the only advertising that's been done is ordering street banners. I'll get ads in the *Journal* right away. Apparently, the funds raised from this one event subsidize most of the group's work for the following year."

"We better not mess up, then." He'd hear it from Cora-Lee for the next twelve months if he did.

Emily gave an emphatic shake of her head. "We're not going to mess up. Not on my shift."

"You know it's a costume event, right?" Chase said.

"That I can handle." She smiled. "It's held in the town hall's community center, correct?"

Chase nodded. "My department always assigns someone for traffic control that evening. I'll find a deputy who wants a little overtime."

"Great. And I checked the booth assignments, and it turns out you rented a booth."

"Cora-Lee did. She wants me to schmooze and pass out swag."

"You're a step ahead of Buster. He probably isn't aware of the opportunity, and his campaign manager isn't local."

"Are you going to tell him?"

Emily shrugged. "There isn't any point. The game booths are assigned to volunteers from the local churches, and all the vendor booths are sold out." She raised a palm. "He won't be happy, but there's nothing you and I can do about it."

"Hold that thought when he complains. And I trust that as your co-chair, you'll let me know what I can do to help."

She smiled. "You'll be the first to know. Right now, everything is in order."

"Thanks for being on top of things, Emily."

"Am I? No, I'm being proactive to avoid being the woman who tanked the town's newspaper *and* the Harvest Festival."

"You're not going to tank the *Journal*. It's all anyone in town is talking about."

"Really?" Her face reflected surprise.

"Yep. Now let's discuss your doorknob."

"Oh, that. Is it loose again? I'll deal with the knob tomorrow. There's a toolbox in the basement."

"Where's the basement?"

"The door is over by the supply room, in back." Emily stood up.

"I've got this covered." He strode across the office and flipped the light to the basement. The cement block steps were as old as Aspen Creek. So was the basement. Brick walls and a cement floor. A vintage printing press sat in one corner and the Beast in another. A small washer and dryer had also been set up in the basement. Though he couldn't remember hearing of anyone else actually living in the apartment upstairs except for Emily, he supposed that at some point, the place had been rented out.

He grabbed the toolbox and headed back upstairs. "What's with the printing press?" he asked.

"That's a Miehle vertical. Used in the '80s. Part and parcel of the deal to buy the paper."

"Why don't you sell it or give it away to a museum?"

"Mostly because I've only been in town three weeks and saving the paper has been my first priority." She looked at him. "Grace mentioned that, too. I'll put it on my to-do list."

Emily glanced at the plant arrangement on the table in the conference room. "Thank you for the plants. A lovely gesture."

"They're from the entire department."

"Then be sure to thank the entire department." Emily paused. "It's only been three weeks, but I'm hoping to get to know more of the town folks. Right now, I only really know a handful of people."

"Give everyone time. Grace and her family have been running the *Journal* since day one. You're an outsider. Half the town is hoping you'll make some changes with the paper. The other half is praying you won't and fully expects you to leave."

"Leave?" She jerked back and studied him. "What do you mean?"

"This is a tourist town. Lots of people come in and set up shop, then get discouraged during the off-season when things are slow."

"I'm not lots of people."

"No, ma'am, you are not." He opened the toolbox and knelt in front of the door. "You made headway at the Soul Sisters meeting. Isn't that something?"

"I suppose so."

He rummaged in the toolbox and found a screwdriver and tightened the screws on the strike plate. Chase stood and rattled the knob to ensure it was secure.

"Thanks for fixing that. You can leave the toolbox there," Emily said. "I'll put it away."

"It may only be a temporary fix." He looked at her for a long minute. "Do me a favor and lock the door at night."

Emily's face softened at the words as though she could read his mind. Could she? If she could, she'd see he cared. And that was problematic.

Emily straightened her wool skirt and added a white silk blouse and tweed blazer. She pulled on black suede boots and assessed herself in the mirror. Conservative and professional. She would be attending the campaign dinner as the press, not a donor.

After combing her hair back into a smooth chignon, she added a simple set of silver chains around her neck and tiny hoops at her ears.

The rhythmic click of nails on the oak floor indicated Byron was on his way from the kitchen to her tiny bedroom. The dog peeked in and did a racing 360 around the room before he stopped to bump his head into her leg.

"What do you think, pal?" She rubbed his silky fur. "Is this outfit going to work?"

The dog wagged his tail and raced in another circle, running right into a small bedside table, knocking her Bible onto the ground.

"Well, that's one way of reminding me to pray before I leave."

Byron was right. She took a deep breath and sat down on the bed.

When she did, Byron jumped up onto a tidy pile of quilts and blankets, settling beside her.

"If you can jump on the bed, why can't you do the stairs?" she asked.

He cocked his head and looked at her. Em placed her hand on his paw before she bowed her head and offered a prayer. "Lord, help me to be discerning and gracious and think before I open my mouth. Amen."

When she stood, Byron inched his way toward the middle of the bed while still on his belly. His big brown eyes reflected love.

Em smiled. This dog was her family now. Byron greeted her each morning, and he was the last thing she saw at the end of each day. The fluffy animal loved her unconditionally. She could have used a few family members like him when she was growing up. Even one would have been nice.

"Thanks, Lord, for bringing Byron into my life."

She petted the pup once more and exited the apartment, making her way downstairs. After locking the offices behind her, Em got into her car and steered her Volkswagen toward the Aspen Creek Inn. The parking lot was full, and so was street parking. She snagged a spot a block away and walked to the building.

Voices and music greeted her as she entered the event room and glanced around, searching for Harley. Red, white and blue was the theme for the evening. The cheerful colors were reflected in floor-to-ceiling balloon pillars, tablecloths and other patriotic decor.

"There you are," Harley said from behind her. Em turned and smiled. "Don't you look like an important person?" She glanced down at herself. "I wore a dress. Is that okay?"

"Of course. You look lovely, Harley."

"Thank you." She twirled, the full skirt of her burgundy dress moving with her, and her strawberry-blond hair bounced with each step. "I picked this up at a little shop in Paradise. Susan's Boutique. She's Bob Jones's daughter."

"I'll have to remember that." Em glanced around, recognizing several women from the Soul Sisters. "The room is full. This is a great sign of support."

"It is, but if you ask me, the man is a shoo-in."

"I hope so." Chase deserved to be reelected, but even more importantly, Sarah would benefit from staying in Aspen Creek. And Em had to selfishly admit that she would be more than okay with both of them being around long-term.

"Is Buster's event really being held in Denver?" Harley asked.

"Yes. Buster doesn't think there are pockets deep enough here in Aspen Creek. And he must be right. His campaign has already raised twice as much as the mayor raised when he ran for office. I checked public records."

"That explains the billboard outside town," Harley said.

"He has a billboard up already?" Em asked.

"Three of them," Moss said as he joined them.

"Hi, Moss," Em said. She turned back to Harley. "Moss is going to Denver to photograph the event. He's meeting a friend of mine I hired to write the story."

"Thanks for taking one for the team, Moss," Harley said. She glanced around. "I'm going to locate our table."

When she left, Moss turned to her. "Emily, I'd like a raise."

She looked up at him. Tonight, he wore a dark suit with a white T-shirt and a white silk pocket square.

"You want a raise."

"Yes. I've worked for the paper for five years. Going to Denver to cover Buster Rutherford is above and beyond. I enjoy my forays into the mile-high city, however, I'm sure you can see that spending time around Buster is suboptimal."

He was right. Absolutely right. There was no way she could manage the paper without Moss and Harley. Unfortunately, there was no money for a raise. Yet.

"I can't afford a raise until we increase the print run, and we'll do that as soon as the paper shows a profit. Until then, I can give you a promotion in title only, like Harley."

He arched a brow.

"How about senior photojournalist? I'll add it to the next edition."

"Senior photojournalist Moss Boutilier." He pursed his lips, thinking. "I like it."

"Where did the name Moss come from?" Em asked.

"Typo. I was supposed to be Moses. Let that be a lesson regarding the power of the pen. Or the computer in this case."

Em smiled. "Well, I prefer Moss," she said.

"Me, too."

He nodded toward the stage. "I'm going to grab my equipment and set up."

"Okay. I know this is a working event, but dinner is free, so take a break to eat."

"Yes, boss."

Harley approached with a huge smile on her face. "I didn't realize that Ryan and the entire Aspen Creek Volunteer Fire Department would be at the sheriff's dinner." She raised her shoulders and clapped her fingertips together.

"Good news?"

"Oh, yes. I haven't been available to take his evening call in two weeks. One night I was home, and I started washing dishes so I could truthfully say I was busy the next time I ran into him."

Em nearly snorted at that. "That's hilarious. Effective but hilarious."

"Are you sure I look all right?" Harley plucked at the skirt of her dress.

"Yes. Of course, he may not recognize you all glamorous. You look amazing, Harley."

"Thank you, Emily." She turned. "Come on. I found our table. It's number six, near the stage."

Em moved to the table and tried to peek at the other place cards. "I wonder who else is at our table."

"Oh, I have an idea. He's heading this way now."

Em started to turn.

"No," Harley hissed. She clamped a hand on Em's arm. "Don't let him know you're looking."

"Who?"

"Three o'clock. Ryan and a few of his friends."

"Why, Harley Augustine. Are we at your table?" Ryan Murphy looked from the ticket in his hand to the place cards on the table. A megawatt smile lit up his face.

"Apparently." She offered a disinterested glance at the cards and looked around the room.

Emily elbowed her.

"Oh, sorry." Harley cleared her throat. "Ryan Murphy, this is my boss, the editor in chief of the *Aspen Creek Journal*, Emily Taylor."

Ryan introduced his friends, who stood next to the table, all chiseled and muscled. And young. Oh, so young.

"They've got a deejay for later," Ryan said, his appreciative gaze on Harley.

Harley smiled. "I heard."

"Will you save me a dance?" Ryan asked.

"I don't know," she hedged. "I've made some promises already."

"One dance?"

"All right, fine." She smiled. "It's the least I can do for an old friend."

"Ouch." Murphy clutched his heart. "That one hurt."

Harley laughed. "You're funny. Now, if you'll excuse me. I see Andy Pickering over there. I should say hello."

"But, Harley..." Ryan followed her, his friends trailing behind.

"Someone's been reading the advice column."

Em turned at Chase's voice. He nodded toward Harley. "Nicely done."

"Me? I didn't do a thing."

"Right." He nodded again and met her gaze, his eyes laughing.

She eyed his crisp blue dress shirt, navy paisley tie and navy suit. He'd shaved, and yet a slight shadow of beard remained. Without a hat on his head, she realized how thick and almost wavy his brown hair was.

"Nice suit," she said.

"Yeah? Cora-Lee made me buy it this week."

"You're supposed to pretend it's no big deal. You have a closet full of suits and tuxes."

Chase chuckled. "I'm an honest man."

Em frowned at his words. *An honest man.* Could he be… No. That was ridiculous.

"You look different tonight," she said.

"Different? How different?" Chase leaned slightly closer, his eyes wide with alarm.

Em cleared her throat. "Handsome." Heat warmed her, circling her neck and moving quickly upward, no doubt flaming her cheeks and ears at the admission.

"Handsome?" Chase chuckled. "You had me worried there." He paused. "How do I usually look?"

"Oh, you know what I mean. Normally, you're all tense and all law enforcement. Tonight, well…you look relaxed."

He laughed again. "Thanks. You look good, too. I like the Lois Lane vibe you have going there."

"Lois Lane, again?" She grimaced. "Really?"

"What? Lois was a serious journalist. And she's cute."

Cute. Chase thought she was cute. She'd mull that later.

Someone tapped the microphone. "Testing. Testing," Cora-Lee boomed. "We'd like everyone to take their seats so our servers can get started with dinner."

"I'll see you later, Emily."

"Not likely, you're at the important-people table."

Chase smiled, the hazel eyes intent. "Oh, I'll find you."

Em shivered at his gaze, her pulse quickening. She turned away and found her seat. A moment later, Harley slid into the chair beside her. Around the table, the handsome firemen also took their seats.

Harley leaned close and lowered her voice. "What were you

and Sheriff Everett talking about? It looked like he was flirting with you."

"Chase? No. We were just talking. I told you. We're friends."

"Emily, that man was not looking at you like you were just friends." She smiled knowingly. "My guess is he'll ask you to dance later."

Em unfolded her napkin and shook her head. "I won't be dancing with anyone. I'm the publisher of the local paper. Eventually the paper has to endorse a candidate. I have to remain unbiased."

"Well, that stinks. I better find out if Ryan has any plans to run for office."

"Who is that woman at the table with Chase?" Em asked. She picked up a program as she slid another look at the gal with the tiara and sparkly dress, leaning way too close to the sheriff.

"The Rio Grande County Cattle Queen. She's from Paradise. We've never had a winner from Aspen Creek. A couple of runners-up, but that's it."

"She looks like she's twelve."

"They keep getting younger and younger." Harley sighed. "You should be sitting at that table. You're the editor in chief of the *Journal*."

"I can take notes for a story here." Although if that beauty queen got any closer to Chase, Em might have to go up to the table and intervene. She blinked at the jealous thought that appeared out of nowhere.

"And why is the mayor up there? His nephew is running against the sheriff."

"I don't know, but I've heard him speak before. Lots of wind." Em eyed the program. "This is going to be a long night."

Six speeches and a yodeling demonstration. All followed by an hour of dancing. Em noted, with a questionable amount of satisfaction, that Chase hadn't danced, either.

Now, three hours later, she was more than ready to head

home. She nudged Harley. "I'm going to slip out. Byron will need to do his thing by now."

"Sure. It'll be over in a few minutes anyhow. Look, Cora-Lee is giving the final words."

"See you on Monday," Em said.

Em pulled the edges of her blazer together against the cold wind as she headed down the street to her car. Beneath the hazy yellow glow of the streetlamps, she could see the flat tire. Well, wasn't that just peachy?

So she'd walk home. It was only a couple of blocks away. Too bad she hadn't brought a coat. A glance up at the sky told her that this might be the night the first flakes fell. She shivered and blew a puff of air. It created a small cloud and then dissipated. Winter was on the way.

"Uh-oh. Looks like a flat."

Em turned around to find Chase standing on the sidewalk. "Good eye, Sheriff. How'd you get out of there so fast?"

"I saw you leave and told Cora-Lee I had to catch you before you left and tell you something important."

"Tell me something important. What?"

"Um..." He shrugged and put his hands in his pockets. "How about that I never want to hold a campaign dinner again?"

She laughed. "Whose idea was the yodeling?"

"Guess."

"Well, she's a great yodeler." Em rubbed her hands together. "Points for that."

"Getting cold out here," Chase observed. He glanced at the tire. "I could change it now or give you a ride home and change it tomorrow."

"Or I could change it now."

"Yeah, that, too. But it is cold, and we're all dressed up."

"True."

"How about a ride home and we can arm wrestle over who changes the tire tomorrow?"

Em laughed. "Yes, please. Thank you."

He pointed farther down the street where his truck was parked, and they started walking.

"I noticed you didn't accept any invitations to dance tonight," Chase said.

"As the head of the local media, it's best if I don't do anything that might make me the next news story." She shrugged. "Besides, I don't want to encourage anyone. I don't have time for a relationship."

"Never?" he asked.

"I don't know about never." Their steps were in sync as they moved beneath the shop canopies of Main Street. "I've always been much too busy working to support myself to think about a relationship. Breaking into media means lots of years of low-level jobs. I waited tables on the side, worked as a delivery person. Anything to pay the bills."

Emily realized she was talking way too much and closed her mouth.

Chase peeked at her from the corner of his eyes. "I apologize, then."

Her head shot up in surprise. "Why?"

"I've misjudged you. Frankly, you always struck me as someone born with a silver spoon in her mouth, so to speak."

"Things are not exactly as they appear," she murmured. The silver spoon had been snatched back the minute she had refused to follow the rules.

"How'd you manage to scrape up the money to buy the *Journal*?"

"I've been saving all my life for an opportunity like this. Then my grandmother pushed me to take a step of faith. She really believed in me. I'm not sure I would have had the courage to do this if not for her."

"I've got a mother like that," Chase said.

"You're very fortunate, then."

"Is she in Denver? Your grandmother?" he asked.

Em glanced at the sidewalk cracks as emotion bubbled up. "No. She passed away last spring. That's why it took me so long to get back to Aspen Creek. She left me her car."

Chase stopped walking, a grimace of pain on his face. "Emily. I'm really sorry."

"Thanks, Chase. The point is, I knew someday I would find my dream. And so did my grandmother." Em smiled. "It helped that Grace was selling the paper for a song and hadn't had what she considered an appropriate offer in months. She wanted to turn the paper over to someone who understood weekly papers."

"That sounds like maybe you were supposed to buy the paper?"

"Exactly. Like part of a divine plan. Do you believe that's possible?"

"Sure do," Chase said. When they reached his truck, he moved to the passenger side and opened the door. The breeze rustled the aspens, and a whiff of Chase's cologne drifted to her. Something warm and comforting. Maybe cedar? He offered her a hand, and she took it, stepping into the vehicle.

"Thank you," she said, liking the feel of her hand in his.

He stared at her hand in his and met her gaze. "I'll turn the heater on."

Chase came around to the other side, buckled his seat belt, started the engine and backed out. "I'm having a hard time believing the *Journal* is anyone's destiny. Especially someone like you."

"What do you mean, like me?" Emily kept her eye on him as she fastened her seat belt.

He shrugged. "You're sort of like a shooting star, vibrant and full of energy. Shooting stars are on their way up."

She stared at him for a moment, stunned by the words. "While that's very flattering, you're way off the mark. My goal in life is much simpler. I want to build something of my own here in Aspen Creek. Dig a little niche, get nice and cozy, and never leave."

"That sounds like you're hiding."

"Not at all. I was searching, and now I've found where I belong. That's not hiding at all. Huge difference."

He nodded, as though thinking. "I guess I'll take your word for it. For now."

"How kind of you," she murmured.

"Hey, I'm a cop. Comes with the territory."

"I'll return the suspicion, of course. Since I am a journalist."

A slow smile crossed Chase's face. "Touché." He pulled the truck into a space directly in front of the *Journal* and offered a smile that made her forget everything for a moment.

"Thank you, Chase. Your support and friendship mean a lot." Emily stopped talking as she recalled her words to Harley. Words she'd repeated again in the advice column. *Friendships provide a foundation for lasting relationships.*

She released a small gasp. No, that was Harley and Ryan. That was different. This was Chase Everett. She barely had time for Byron, much less the sheriff of Aspen Creek.

"Emily? You okay?"

She blinked and turned to him. Confusion was in his eyes, a crooked smile on his mouth as he looked back at her.

"Yes. Sorry. Thinking."

"Looked like you were having an argument with yourself."

"Did it?" She paused. Maybe she was. "Sorry. I've got a lot on my mind."

"You sure that's all?"

"Yes. I'm sure."

Chase opened his door and walked around to the passenger side.

A lot on her mind. Emily shook her head once more. Now, that was an understatement. Now she could add falling for the sheriff to her list. That took her completely by surprise.

He opened the passenger door and helped her down again. "Let me walk you to your door. Front door or around to the back?"

"This is fine." She paused on the sidewalk and looked up. Overhead, fat, lazy flakes rode the breeze moving toward them. Em stood staring into the night. "Chase. It's snowing."

He glanced up and smiled. "First flakes. Do you know who won?"

"No, we have names in envelopes for each date from last Tuesday through to the end of December. We'll draw a name from those who chose the correct date." She laughed as they danced through the sky. "Do you remember eating the first flakes when you were a kid?"

"Ah, no, but my sister did that. She'd twirl around on the lawn, jumping up and eating the flakes."

"Good memories," Em said on a sigh. She followed Chase to the door.

He nodded. "The best."

"I'd have liked to have a sister."

"No siblings?"

"Oh, I have six or seven stepbrothers."

"That many? Where's your father?"

"Who knows? We don't talk." Em paused and grimaced. "It's complicated."

Chase nodded. "How long since you've seen him?"

"Oh, at least five years. I do talk to him on occasion, though mostly I dodge his calls." She raised a hand. "Again. Complicated."

"Have you thought about finding a way to uncomplicate things? Maybe agree to disagree?"

"I've tried before, and he steps over the line every time." She released a breath. "Besides, you don't know my father. He takes the oxygen out of a room. It's his way or the highway. I lose who I am when I'm around him." She'd nearly lost herself to his fake fiancé as well.

He shrugged. "Maybe things have changed in five years. People do change, Emily."

"Maybe so." She looked at him. "You're right. I won't rule it out."

Chase chuckled.

Em frowned. "What's so funny?"

"I've been standing beneath the awning. You've got flakes all over your hair." He reached out and brushed them off.

Em froze at his nearness, and then his hand stopped. Chase stared at her and leaned closer. His lips barely touched hers. It was a kiss so light that she could have imagined it. But she didn't. There was no way she imagined the way her heart skittered, her breathing nearly stopped.

"Good night, Emily. Lock the door, please."

"Yes. Yes. I will."

Her hand trembled as she unlocked the door and stepped inside. She carefully locked it behind her then walked slowly to the back stairs.

Chase Everett had kissed her.

First flakes. First kiss from Chase Everett.

First time she'd have to consider that she might be falling in love with him.

Chapter Nine

"When will Grandma be back?" Sarah asked. She pushed her cereal around in the bowl, then sat back in her chair with a pained sigh.

"Soon." He finished the remains of his coffee, put the mug on the table and watched his niece. Silence filled the kitchen, the only sound the birds chirping in the backyard.

"I miss my mom." The whispered words came out on a sob, knifing straight into Chase's heart. Turning to Sarah, he pulled her onto his lap and rubbed her back as she silently cried. "I miss her, too," he said softly.

Next month would be a year, and the pain hadn't shown signs of easing. He could distract himself from thinking about Phoebe's death by working long hours, but the ache appeared when he least expected it. It was probably even worse for his niece.

Chase didn't have anything else to say to comfort Sarah. To comfort himself.

He wasn't a man with flowery speeches who could dispense the wisdom of Bible verses at the drop of a hat. Yet, he did his best to trust the Lord, even when he didn't understand why life could be so unfair.

If his mother were here, she'd know what to do, but she was still in Denver. Here it was Saturday, a week since the campaign dinner, and between his day job and campaigning, life had only become busier. He'd adjusted his work schedule to get home by four each day but hadn't managed to get to the dog park so Sarah could see Byron and Emily.

He'd kissed the woman and then hadn't seen her in a week. *Yeah, not good, Chase.* The truth was he didn't know what to do about how he felt about Emily. He shouldn't have kissed her, but he had. That kiss had replayed in his mind more than once of late.

Still. It wasn't fair to her.

What would happen once she found out who he really was? The shame of his past would never go away. It was like a stain that you couldn't remove.

All he could do now was apologize. Not only was it the right thing to do, but the bottom line was that he was the parent in training, and this was more about Sarah than himself. He could only pray Emily would forgive him—for his niece's sake.

"How about if we go over to Emily's and see if she and Byron want to come out to play with us?"

Sarah lifted her head from his chest and searched his face, her eyes watery with emotion. "Oh, yes, please."

"Okay. Go wash your face and get ready. We'll go see Emily and Byron."

She nodded. "Thank you, Uncle Chase."

"Grab your hat and mittens, too. It's a little frosty out there."

Chase glanced at the clock. Seven o'clock. He hoped Emily was a morning person. A morning person who didn't hold a grudge.

Less than thirty minutes later, he parked the truck outside the *Journal* offices. "Stay right here," he told Sarah.

He got out of the truck and looked for a doorbell or a buzzer. There wasn't one. He should have called first, but he'd feared she wouldn't answer. Chase walked around the corner and looked up at the window on the second floor. Searching the ground, he found a nice round stone and tossed it at the pane.

Immediately, the sash flew up, and Emily stuck her head out the window.

"Am I in trouble again? That parking spot clearly says after five during the week and on weekends." She paused her tirade and shot him a fierce glance. "It's the weekend."

"Good morning to you, too." Chase smiled. It was good to see her face, even if she was frowning. "I'm not here to give you a ticket." He looked down at his clothes. "I'm not in uniform."

"Then why are you here?"

"I'm wondering what you're up to this morning," he replied.

"Right now, I'm shivering because the window is open." She paused as if considering the situation. "You know, most people call or text to ask what I'm up to."

"Like you, I'm not most people."

"That's the truth." She gave a short laugh. "I'm about to run errands and knock off my to-do. I've got a list of supplies I promised to pick up for the Harvest Festival."

"I'm supposed to help you with that."

"It's not a big deal. The hardware store should have everything." She looked at him. "You didn't come all the way over here to ask what I'm up to. Why are you here throwing stones at my window?"

"Sarah and I want to know if you and Byron can come out and play."

Emily glanced around suspiciously. "Where's Sarah?"

"In the truck."

She frowned. "I'll be right down. See you at the office door."

"Is that a yes?" he called.

"It's a 'see you at the door.'"

Relieved, Chase walked back around the corner, opened the back seat of the truck and helped Sarah out of her booster seat.

"Did she say yes?" Sarah asked, her expression hopeful.

"I think so. Come on."

Emily waited for them on the other side of the glass door in jeans and a sweater, her hair in a high ponytail. Yeah, she looked good, and he should have found time to stop by this week. His heart hammered, telling him that forgetting about that kiss was not going to happen.

She held the door and smiled at his niece without sparing a glance at him. "Good morning, Sarah. I've missed seeing you. How are you?"

"Okay."

The offices were toasty warm, Chase noted. The furnace must have been replaced last week.

Sarah walked around the space, peeking curiously into each room. "Where's Byron?"

"Upstairs. My apartment is upstairs. I'll have to get him."

"Could I call him?"

Emily cocked her head and frowned. Then she smiled. "Sure. Let's do that. Follow me."

Chase followed Emily and Sarah down the hall. She opened a door that revealed a staircase. "Byron," she called. "You have a visitor."

The dog whined and appeared at the landing.

"Go ahead and call him," she instructed Sarah.

Sarah clapped her hands together. "Byron. Here, boy. Here, boy."

Byron whined and raced in a circle. He repeated the dance two more times. Finally, he took the first step, looked back at the landing, and then at Sarah.

"Good boy, Byron," Sarah called.

One step. The room was silent as though everyone held their breath.

"Good boy, Byron," Sarah crooned, repeating the praise.

Another step and then another. At the bottom, he leaped into Sarah's arms, knocking her onto her backside.

"You okay, Sarah?" Chase asked.

"Uh-huh." Sarah laughed over and over as Byron licked her face. "Good boy."

Chase couldn't believe what he was seeing.

He looked over at Emily. She sniffed and swiped at her eyes. Her glance flitted to him and then away.

"I've missed you, Emily," he whispered.

She looked at him and shrugged. "I've been right here."

"Where are we going now, Uncle Chase?" Sarah rolled over and got to her feet.

"Anywhere you like."

"I want to go to breakfast. I'm starving."

"Me, too," Emily said.

"Can we take Byron to breakfast?" he asked.

"I have an idea," Emily said. "Let's go to Four Forks. I can get my supplies there, and I hear they have a farmers market on Saturdays. We can get breakfast to go and then check out the market and get Sarah a pumpkin, too. It is October now."

"What do you think, Sarah?" he asked.

"Yes, please."

"Let me get my coat and Byron's leash and water dish." When she started up the stairs, Byron followed, as though he did it all the time. Emily laughed and raced up the steps faster.

Once they were settled in the truck and on the road, Chase checked his rearview mirror. Byron rested on the seat in his harness, with a paw on Sarah, who was buckled in. He hadn't seen her this happy in a very long time.

He glanced at Emily. A smile curved her mouth.

"What are you thinking about?" he asked.

"I'm tickled I don't have to carry Byron up and down steps anymore."

Chase nodded. "Look, um, Emily. I'm sorry this week got away from me."

"You don't have any obligation to me," she said. "Though it would have been nice to see Sarah at the park."

"What if I want an obligation?" he asked. The words popped out, surprising him.

She blinked, turning her head to stare at him, confusion in her eyes. "You mean friends, right?"

"You wanted to go to Four Forks to avoid gossip, didn't you?" he asked.

Emily glanced away. "I don't want to compromise my job or your candidacy."

"How will that happen if we're just friends?"

Friends. That was what he wanted, right? Being around Emily had him tossing common sense out the window.

Emily smiled slowly and turned her attention out the window. "Is there still a Waffle Stop in Four Forks?"

He laughed. "Yep. Still there, and they have a drive-through window."

"Good. I'm very hungry, so I hope you brought your wallet."

"Am I paying?"

"Oh, you absolutely are going to pay."

Chase smiled, his heart warm. He didn't know what was going on here, except that being around Emily seemed like all he'd ever wanted and never dreamed he could have. And if all he got was a day with her and Sarah and Byron, well, he would be grateful.

Em glanced at the perfectly shaped pumpkin in the middle of the conference table, then at the dry-erase board and the calendar. The Harvest Festival was this Saturday. Only two days away. Thanksgiving would be here soon. And the election. She'd been counting the days until the campaign was over and life in Aspen Creek would return to normal.

She smiled and fiddled with the plastic bracelet on her wrist while she recalled Saturday. Breakfast in the park. Sarah and Byron had run all over while she and Chase sat on a bench and watched. Chase and Byron had waited in the truck while she and Sarah went into the big-box store for Harvest Festival supplies.

Once inside the store, they had detoured to the beauty aisle and picked up elastic hair bands so Em could braid Sarah's hair. The little girl had confided that Chase was all thumbs in that department. On impulse, Em grabbed two pink friendship bracelets. One for her and one for Sarah. The child had been thrilled.

The farmers market was huge. The largest market she'd been to in a while. By the time they'd stopped at every vendor's booth, sampling pastries and purchasing produce, they were full and exhausted. When Chase reached out and held her hand, she let him. Around noon, they walked back to the truck, Chase carrying Sarah, who was too tired to walk. A canvas bag filled with produce dangled from his arm. Em hauled two pumpkins and Byron's leash.

"Fresh pot," Harley announced. She placed a mug on the table.

The aroma of coffee roused Em from her daydreams.

"Thank you," she said.

"Where did you get that pumpkin?" Harley asked.

"The farmers market in Four Forks."

"Oh, I love that market."

"Me, too." Em leaned back in her chair and reached for the mug. "Have you heard any feedback on yesterday's paper?"

"Not so much on the paper as on Buster and his campaign event in Denver," Harley said. "Lots of folks have commented on it, and not in a good way. He's alienating the locals."

"Maybe that's a good thing," Em murmured.

"Mail's here," Moss called out. He wore a fur-lined trapper hat with ear flaps dangling and a blue worsted wool coat. After handing over a stack of letters, he placed a box squarely in front of her on the conference table. "Here you go."

Em cut through the packing tape with scissors and folded back the edges of the box to reveal a thick book and a letter.

"Is that a dictionary?" Harley asked.

"It is." Em unfolded the letter and smiled. The author had used a typewriter. "It's from the former principal of Aspen Creek High School." She looked up at Harley. "We spelled *acknowledgment* wrong in the last edition."

"Oh my goodness. I am so sorry. I proofed it."

"Harley. We're human. It happens. The important thing is that they're reading us." She lifted the dictionary from the box. "And this will make a very nice doorstop."

Harley chuckled.

"Shall we start going through this mail?" Em asked. "I'll take the bills if you'll open the rest."

"Sure."

Em handed her a stack and sighed. "I was sort of hoping my pile would be smaller." She tore open the bill from the printer. "Printing costs are going up starting next month." She looked at Harley. "What do you think about raising the price of the *Journal*?"

"This would be the time to do that. It's flying off the shelves at the shops in town. Subscriptions are up. There were people waiting for me last week when I dropped off papers at the barbershop."

"I checked our numbers last week." Em nodded, pleased that they'd been increasing. "This is all good. What are we doing right, do you suppose?"

Harley laughed. "Emily, it's that column. The first topic of discussion when it comes to the paper is *Dispatches from the Heart*."

"They haven't figured out I'm the columnist, have they?"

"Oh, there's lots of speculation. But it's your mystery man that has all the attention. Especially the women in town. They love that he's continued to write letters."

"'An honest man,'" Em mused. She continued to have a niggling suspicion that it was Chase, though it seemed out of character for a man of few words.

"What does Ryan say?" Em asked.

"I think he's jealous because of all the attention the guy is getting. His theory is that it's not even a man. The other blaze busters say that no guy would pen a letter."

"Strong opinions will keep our readers coming back. What do the letters look like this week?" Em asked.

Harley put two on the table. "These will work. One is a mother-in-law problem, the other is a coworker with hygiene issues." She shook her head. "How do you come up with the responses, Emily?"

"Common sense. No more. No less."

Harley opened another envelope and scanned the contents. She frowned. "Oh, my. This one is a little scary. She's afraid her husband will hurt her."

"Oh, no." Em reached for the letter and read it quickly, her hands trembling. "Oh, this is terrible. That poor woman. I should report this to Chase."

"You don't know who it is. What can he do?"

"I have to do something. I'll make a copy and turn it over to him so it's on file."

"And how will you respond to that woman's letter for the *Journal*?"

"I won't print the letter, but I will address the topic in the column by providing resources and encouraging anyone encountering domestic violence to get out of the situation and seek help. That's all I can do."

"It's good to know the paper is providing an outreach."

"Yes." Em sighed, still disturbed by the letter. "I'm going to run a copy of that letter over to the sheriff's office right now. I've got a bad feeling about this. A very bad feeling." She glanced at the clock. "Would you lock up before you head to the library?"

"Sure thing. Let me know what the sheriff says."

"I will." Em grabbed her coat, headed out the door and race-walked down Main to the sheriff's office building, her thoughts in turmoil.

When she opened the door, the first thing she saw was Cora-Lee seated at a long table sorting items into small bags.

"What are you up to, Cora-Lee?" she asked.

"Oh, good morning, Emily. These are the swag bags the sheriff will give away at his booth."

"What a great idea."

"I thought so."

Em glanced at Chase's closed office door. "Is the sheriff available?"

Cora-Lee stood. "Sure is. Let me buzz him." She moved to her desk and pushed a button. "Sheriff, Emily Taylor is here to see you."

Chase's door opened and he smiled. "Did we have an appointment I forgot about again?"

"No. I thought I'd throw a stone and see what you were up to."

His lips twitched. "Come on in." He shut the door and looked at her. "Good to see you, Emily. Real good."

Em blushed. "You, too. Thanks for making it to the dog park this week."

"I'm trying. I've asked Cora-Lee to cut back on my campaign schedule. Sarah comes first." He slipped behind his desk and turned on a fan before sitting down.

"Are you warm?"

"White noise. The fan keeps Cora-Lee out of my business."

"Oh, good idea." She handed him the envelope she'd received and sat down.

He read the letter and turned the envelope over. "Postmarked Aspen Creek. You aren't going to print this, are you?"

"I'll address the topic without printing the letter. We can

provide resources and suggest readers in this situation create a safety plan and contact your office."

"Yeah, that's perfect. You'll get that in the next edition?"

"Yes." She searched his face. "Do you know who this might be?"

"I have a few thoughts I'll check into and have my deputies ask around quietly as well."

"I'm heartbroken that someone in town is going through this and her only recourse is a letter to the newspaper."

Concern washed over Chase's face. He folded his arms and looked at her. "Promise me you'll lock the office doors when you're alone."

"I do. Why are you worried about me? I'm not going to print the letter."

"Doesn't matter. The *Journal* just became involved in this woman's domestic issues, and that could very well trigger responses. The wrong kind."

He paused. "Remember, Emily. You are the face of the paper."

"That doesn't make any sense. I'm offering help."

"It doesn't have to make sense. If someone believes there are two sides and the paper is interfering by posting resources." Chase raised his palms.

"I don't agree with your assessment."

"I didn't say it made sense." He paused. "Just use caution. Please."

His gaze met hers, and she sucked in a breath at what she saw. Chase was more than worried.

"I will."

"Sheriff, come quick, it's important," Cora-Lee called.

Both Em and Chase turned at her voice.

"Uh-oh," Chase muttered. He raced around his desk and yanked open the door. "What is it?"

Eyes wide, Cora-Lee shook her head. "You won't believe

it. I just got a call from the Denver Police. Buster Rutherford's been arrested and charged with fraud."

Em's mouth dropped open at the announcement.

"Who did you talk to?" Chase asked.

"Community liaison something or other. He's going to email you." She paused. "Does this mean the election is over?"

"Not hardly. Buster is innocent until proven guilty. Besides, he's a write-in candidate. Nothing changes even if he wins the election until he withdraws or is deemed disqualified by the town council."

Em looked from Cora-Lee to Chase. "I've got to go call my sources in Denver and get this in the next edition of the *Journal*." She looked at Chase. "Thanks for handling that other matter."

"That's my job. Remember what I said."

"Oh, I doubt I can forget it," she murmured. She stepped out onto the sidewalk. The sunshine had disappeared, and an ominous cloud hung over the town. A shiver raced over her.

It seemed as though all she'd done for the last five weeks was look for news. Today, the news had chased her down. Em hurried her steps, a silent prayer on her lips for the woman who wrote that letter.

Chapter Ten

Kettle corn. Em nodded as she identified the smell. The air in the community center was thick with the sweet scent, causing her stomach to grumble.

Around her, the crowded room was abuzz with laughter and the sound of children running amok. Em gripped Sarah's hand and moved past the crowd entering the room, to the perimeter where there were fewer people. She greeted several of the Soul Sisters responsible for the Harvest Festival. They were the real heroes who'd made the event possible. She and Chase hadn't done much more than supervise.

Sarah tugged at Em's sleeve, and she looked down at the little girl dressed like a puppy dog with long felt ears and a painted brown nose. Em grinned. She and Chase had put together the outfit last night at his house, creating the getup using footed pajamas. The result was an adorable—and somber—puppy dog. Em had offered to take Sarah to the festival, knowing he would be campaigning. She enjoyed hanging out with Sarah and was appreciative of their growing friendship.

"Emily, look. That's my mailman."

Em followed the direction Sarah's paw pointed. Sure enough, across the room, she spotted Moss. He'd draped what looked like white sheets over himself, clipped them at the shoulders with clothespins. Moss carried a 3-D–printed version of the

Ten Commandments in the crook of one arm, while his camera hung from around his neck.

"What's his costume?" Sarah asked.

"Moses from the Bible."

Sarah screwed up her face.

"It's a very loose interpretation." She smiled at Sarah's reaction. "Come on. Let's go find your uncle. He's here somewhere."

They'd taken a few steps when Em heard a familiar voice. "Edna! Is that you?"

Em turned around. "Hi, Minnie." The Soul Sister's hair seemed a bit more lavender today, and she'd donned a different pair of red cat-eye glasses. These were adorned with rhinestones.

"What a cute dog," Minnie said. She patted Sarah on the head and assessed Em. "What are you?"

"Lois Lane. See my press pass?" Em offered Minnie a look at the badge that hung around her neck by a lanyard. She didn't bother to mention the obvious pencil skirt, blazer, sturdy shoes and a circa-1950s pillbox hat, found at the local thrift shop.

Minnie leaned closer, squinting. "*Daily Planet.*" She chuckled, a gloved hand over her mouth. "I get it now."

"Have you seen the sheriff?" Em asked. "I did a walk-through this morning, before the festival doors opened. His booth was over by the beverage table then." She pointed to the right. "But the Happy Trails Scouts are there now, selling popcorn."

Minnie gave a thoughtful nod. "I guess Cora-Lee moved him. You should find her."

"I'll do that."

"Emily, who was that?" Sarah asked.

"That was Minnie. She came as herself."

"Why did she call you Edna?"

"I'm not sure, but it's okay."

Sarah nodded, once again looking confused.

"Are you hungry?" Em asked when a couple walked by with cinnamon nuts. She was definitely getting hungry.

"No. Uncle Chase made pancakes this morning."

"Pancakes? Again? That Uncle Chase sure is a good uncle." Pancakes sounded wonderful. "Okay, then. Let's keep going. We'll find your uncle. Then we can play some games."

"Hey, Lois Lane! Slow down. I can't walk in these sandals."

Em started laughing when she saw who was clomping behind her. Harley, in an oversize brown bathrobe, with a head wrap and an impressive beard. She carried a staff and a large stuffed lamb. "Are those Birkenstocks on your feet?"

"Uh-huh. I borrowed them from my dad. They're a little clumsy and a couple sizes too big." She blew beard hair away from her mouth and smiled. "You two look awesome."

"Sarah, this is my friend Harley."

"I know her," Sarah said. "From the library." She assessed Harley's costume carefully. "She's a shepherd." Sarah sounded relieved to be able to identify Harley.

"Yes. She is."

"Thank you, Sarah," Harley said. "Minnie thought I was a member of a British rock band."

Em's lips twitched.

"Have you seen Ryan?" Harley asked.

"I noticed the volunteer fire department reserved a booth to pass out fire safety material and candy. But he wasn't at the booth. What's he dressed as?"

"Oh, he came as a handsome firefighter." She grinned, then her face sobered. She leaned forward and lowered her voice. "Have you heard anything more about Buster?"

"No. I think our coverage in the *Journal* was very kind, but we'll see what people say when the paper comes out next week." She shrugged. "Cora-Lee said the mayor is very upset. He's not going to make an appearance today."

"Oh, that's too bad. But I get it. When my little brother

got caught with his hand in the donation bucket at church, my mother refused to attend service for a month. She was humiliated."

"Yes, but Buster isn't twelve."

"No?" Harley raised her brows, and her beard wiggled. "I'll see you two later."

"She's funny," Sarah said.

"Yes, she is," Em agreed. She took Sarah's hand again and wove around the line for face painting. "Do you want your face painted? We can get in line. It's moving quickly."

Sarah grimaced. "No, thank you."

The child had excellent taste. No way would she pay good money for a stranger to paint a sparkly pink unicorn on her cheek.

"Look. There's Uncle Chase." Sarah released Em's hand and raced up to a red, white and blue booth.

Sheriff Chase Everett in a crisp uniform, with a cowboy hat, stood behind a rectangular table draped with red, white and blue bunting and filled with swag bags and bumper stickers. Em's heart danced when he smiled at her.

Then he came around the table and stood next to Em, frowning at Sarah. "How did this puppy get into the community center, Emily?"

Sarah laughed. "It's me, Uncle Chase."

"Oh, Sarah. I forgot it was a costume. You look like a real dog."

She shook her head, clearly disillusioned with the adult population today. Then she walked into Chase's booth and sat in his chair. "May I have a treat bag?"

"Sure." Chase looked at Emily. "May I interest you in a treat bag?"

"What's in the bag?"

"I have no idea and I am terrified to find out."

"I'll take an Everett for Sheriff bumper sticker, then."

"Wise choice." He smiled. "I see you have your Lois Lane vibe going again."

"You inspired my costume. Besides, there's a lot to like about Lois."

"You don't have to convince me. I agree. She's independent, intelligent, attractive and strong-willed."

"Did you just call me stubborn?"

He laughed. "Have I thanked you for bringing Sarah to the festival?"

"As the co-chair who did next to nothing, I'm happy to support this very successful event."

"Yeah, funny thing about the assignment. I've come to the conclusion that Cora-Lee may be gaslighting us as part of a master plan to get us to volunteer for the Christmas extravaganza. Lulling us into believing it's all easy-peasy. Next thing you know, we're dressed as elves baking cookies for the entire town."

"You do have a top-of-the-line oven." Em smiled and cocked her head. "Would it be so bad wearing tights and green felt suits?"

Chase chuckled. "I'd do it with you, Emily."

Her face warmed at his words and the tenderness in his eyes.

"Do what?"

Em whirled around at the sound of Hope's voice.

"Grandma! You're back." Sarah raced to hug her grandmother.

"Yes, my little puppy dog, I just got back in town. Emily, dear. You're a perfect Lois Lane."

"Thank you, Hope. Good to see you." It was good to see Chase's mother, though Em couldn't help but note how tired she appeared.

"Hey, Mom, you doing okay?" Chase put an arm around his mother and kissed the top of her head.

"I am. My friend is better, and we've bumped the cruise up to November."

"Good for you. Glad to hear it."

"I heard about Buster." Hope shook her head in dismay. "We can discuss that later."

"Nothing much to talk about," Chase said. "The election is unchanged at this point."

A couple stepped up to Chase's booth, and Hope nodded toward them.

"We'll talk to you later, dear," she said. "Come along, Sarah. Uncle Chase is busy." Hope put her arm through Em's as they walked toward the festival games. "Thank you so much for helping Chase."

"I haven't done much."

"That's not what he says. I heard about the sprinkles, and you've already picked out a pumpkin, and Sarah and Byron have had quality time. I'm grateful."

Sarah moved to stand between the adults. She looked from her grandmother to Em. "May I play that?" She pointed to a fish-in-a-barrel game.

"Sure," Hope said. "Get in line. We'll wait right here."

"You need tickets," Em said. She tore six tickets off a roll and handed them to Sarah.

As they stood watching, Hope moved closer to Em. "It's so nice to see you and Chase getting close."

"We're co-chairs of the event."

"Yes. Yes. But my son really likes you."

Em froze. While there was no denying that something was indeed happening between them, it was something new and fragile, and Em wasn't sure she wanted to share it with the world, election or no election.

"I, um… We're friends," Em offered.

"Oh, it's more than that. A mother knows these things." Hope smiled. "It's a big deal because Chase is always careful not to put himself in a position to be hurt again. He's learned over the years that people are always willing to believe the worst."

Confused, Em looked at Hope. Her hazel eyes, so much like Chase's, reflected pain.

"My son carries a burden that isn't his to carry. It's actually mine, except I turned things over to the Lord years ago. I haven't convinced Chase to do that yet."

"I don't understand."

"Yes, I know, but at some point, you will, and then I want you to promise me that you'll remember this conversation."

Em said nothing, only nodded and looked over at Chase's booth where he chatted with voters and passed out swag. She couldn't figure out what Hope was trying to tell her, but she suspected she was going to find out very soon.

The two-story log cabin was hidden behind a row of conifers. Chase parked the patrol car in the gravel drive and walked up the stone path to the house. Ever since the incident three weeks ago, he had asked his deputies to drive by the place more often. Since the anonymous letter that he strongly suspected had been penned by Dolly Towers, and the subsequent advice appeared in yesterday's paper, Chase decided it would be good to do a wellness check.

The exterior of the Towerses' home was tidy, with an autumn wreath on the door. Everything appeared fine on the outside, but Chase knew too well how deceiving appearances could be. His stepfather had seemed to be an all-right guy, until his mother married him.

Chase knocked, but there was no response. He got back in his car and called his admin. Cora-Lee was privy to the situation. When it came to her job, she could be trusted to be discreet.

"Yes, Sheriff?"

"Have you heard anything on Dolly Towers?"

"I reached out to a friend of hers a short time ago. She's

taken the advice in the *Journal*, and left to stay with a relative in another state." Cora-Lee paused. "And, Sheriff, she admitted she wrote the letter. Doesn't want to press charges, but she wants Ennis to get help."

"Does Ennis know where she is?"

"What I'm hearing is no, and he's furious. Been calling all her friends and raising a fuss."

"Any idea what set him off?"

"Lost his job, I hear."

"That's too bad," Chase said with a slow nod. "Thanks, Cora-Lee. Do me a favor and encourage her friends to call 9-1-1 if they feel threatened. In the meantime, I'll keep trying to locate him. Maybe he and I can have a chat."

"Yes, sir. I will."

Chase ended the call with a heavy sense of foreboding. But there wasn't anything he could do except be alert.

Twenty years ago, he'd said the same words to himself. *Stay alert, Chase. Something is going to happen.*

And it had.

Chase gave the house one last look before he headed into town. Maybe he'd swing by the *Journal* and talk to Emily. He hadn't seen her since the Harvest Festival on Saturday. Could he be missing the feisty journalist?

He parked the truck outside the newspaper office and headed toward the door.

A group of women departed the office as he approached.

"Congratulations on your endorsement," one woman said.

"Thank you." He'd nearly forgotten the endorsement was in Tuesday's paper. The *Aspen Creek Journal* had officially endorsed him. That would go a long way toward garnering votes.

Several more women exited. Holding the door for them, he noticed the entire knob, lock and dead bolt had been replaced. He nodded his approval.

"Hello, Sheriff Everett," Emily said. She circled a large folding table with a trash can, tidying up what looked like the remains of a party.

"I see your door hardware has been replaced."

"When I bought a new lock, Ryan Murphy threw in a new dead bolt for half price. He volunteered to do the work free of charge as well. I'm pretty sure it was an opportunity to talk to Harley that prompted the offer."

"I would have done it for you."

"You're the sheriff. I can't bother you with office repairs. Your job is to nag me about the lock, that's all." She smiled. A simple smile that touched his heart.

"Glad I nagged you into replacing them, but you can bother me anytime. I'm always happy to help." Chase smiled back, enjoying their easy repartee. He glanced around the reception area and sniffed the air. "I smell cake."

"Pineapple-carrot cake from the bakery. They're in cute little individual containers in the fridge. Help yourself." She put the trash can down and added more napkins and plastic utensils to the table.

"What's the occasion?"

"You suggested an open house. I took the idea and ran with it. Our space is somewhat limited, as you can see, so I scheduled several small open house events and sent out invitations. We just concluded one for local business owners. I have another scheduled in an hour, and a final one on Monday."

He nodded and stepped over to the reception table and smiled at the basket of pens and magnets. "I see you took a page from Cora-Lee with the swag."

"What can I say? A good idea is worth emulating. I had pens and refrigerator magnets printed with our email, tip-line number and our website address."

"You're amazing, Emily."

"I have my moments. Thanks for noticing."

Again, he glanced around. "Where's your staff?" Usually

Moss worked in the afternoons and Harley the mornings. Chase wasn't a fan of Emily being alone in the office.

"Moss will be back soon, and Harley just left for the library." She glanced at the clock. "I'll get some work done before Byron and I meet your mom and Sarah at the park."

"What do you think about dinner tonight?"

She stopped moving and looked at him, eyes rounded. "You and me?"

"Yeah. You and me." He smiled, warmed by her response. "There's a nice place in Four Forks we could try."

Emily stared at him for a minute. "I'd like that," she said softly. "Any particular reason?"

Chase realized he could offer a dozen reasons why he wanted to sit across a table and stare into her dark eyes. Instead, he said, "Does there have to be?"

"I guess not."

"By the way, thank the publisher for the endorsement," he said.

"You were always the candidate of choice for the *Journal*, you know. With jury selection going on around Buster and his former firm, it seemed an appropriate time to make the call."

"Still, I appreciate it."

"The publisher says thank you." She smiled. "Now, how about a sit-down with the paper to discuss your long-term plans? I'd like to come up with something a little more personal than the last article."

"Is that necessary?"

She cocked her head. "I would think you'd be eager for the publicity."

"I don't think anyone cares. And why do I need more publicity? I had a fund-raising dinner. There's a goofy billboard out on the highway. I passed out bumper stickers and got some airtime." The topic was making him cranky, and he knew it.

A wise man would change the subject, but he felt compelled to make a point.

"Surely you don't think that's what a campaign is all about?" Surprise flared in Emily's eyes.

"Absolutely not. This is Aspen Creek. What I think is that no one cares about that stuff, and they don't care much about what I have to say, either. They care about what I do. And I've been doing fine for four years."

"I'm going to keep pressing you, you know."

"Do what you have to do, Emily. I understand that it's your job."

Emily put a hand on his arm and smiled sweetly. "Thank you."

When she smiled, he lost his train of thought for a moment.

"Um… You're welcome."

"Have you heard any follow-up regarding the domestic violence resources we printed in the paper?" she asked.

"Nothing I can talk about right now." He checked his watch. "I'll pick you up at six. Will that work?"

"Make it six thirty." She hesitated and met his gaze. "I'm looking forward to it."

"Me, too," he murmured. Chase left the *Journal*, smiling.

A mere six weeks ago, he'd savored solitude. Emily Taylor had changed that. He'd come to understand that being alone was an excuse to avoid taking a chance. No guts, no glory, as Sheriff Flanagan used to say.

He had to take a chance. Tonight he'd explain, off the record, what had happened twenty years ago. And maybe she'd understand.

Unable to shake an uneasy feeling, Chase stood on the sidewalk for a moment, glancing up and down Main. Nothing seemed amiss. Outside the barbershop, Liam gestured while in an animated conversation with a customer. A horn honked as

Ryan Murphy ran across the street, jaywalking again. Nothing unusual there.

Chase got in his patrol car and started down Main Street. At the traffic light, he scanned the perimeter. He spotted Minnie entering the bakery. A few doors down, an older gentleman stepped out of a dark Lexus parked at the curb and walked into the pharmacy.

Chase froze.

Though he could only see the man in profile, he recognized him immediately. Yeah, he could still identify the man who'd tried to put him away for life. Chase's grip tightened on the steering wheel, and his jaw clenched. He willed himself to relax, as his mind scrambled for an answer.

Douglas Baker was in Aspen Creek. His past had found him.

Chapter Eleven

"Emily, I'm so glad you invited us. This was an inspired idea," Lucy Reynolds said. "I've enjoyed hearing about your vision for the paper."

"I agree," a pretty redhead said. "And I appreciate that you're interested in the community's input as well."

The chairs had been arranged in a semicircle in the *Journal*'s lobby, making it easier for Emily to read the name tags she'd provided for her guests. She eyed the name of the redhead who had just spoken. Jett Stephens from the bakery. The woman who baked the delicious carrot cakes.

"I always thought it might be fun to see a feature in the paper about small towns," Sloane Flanagan said.

"What do you mean?" Emily asked.

"Oh, you know, like that comedy guy on television does. Except call it, 'You Might Live in a Small Town If…'"

Jett laughed. "Oh, I love that idea."

"Me, too," several other guests chimed in at the same time.

Em turned to Moss, who'd offered to take meeting notes. She couldn't help but notice his attention had been on Sloane most of the meeting. "Did you catch that, Moss?"

"Got it. Great idea, Sloane." He nodded and scribbled on a legal pad.

Sloane blushed at the praise.

Emily glanced at the clock and stood. It was time to end

things so she could get to the park. "Be sure to take a magnet and pen before you leave," she said to the group. "The paper's number is there, along with our website."

Shortly after the group departed, Harley arrived.

"Aren't you supposed to be at the library?" Em asked.

"Someone forgot to tell me it's closed. They're replacing the carpets. I thought I'd catch up here since I took time off this morning." She looked around. "How did the open house events go?"

"Really well, right, Moss?"

"I enjoyed it." He looked toward the front door. "I think I'll go over to the House of Tea and chat with Sloane about that great idea of hers."

"Have fun," Em murmured as he left.

"What idea?" Harley asked.

"I'll tell you later. I have to get going. It's almost time to meet Sarah at the park." Then she had to get ready to meet Chase for dinner. Em glanced at the big wall clock, excited for the evening plans.

"Where's Byron?" Harley asked.

"I had to lock him in my bedroom. He's not happy." Em glanced at the clock again as she grabbed a trash can. "I'll go get him."

"Why don't I clean up for you?"

"That would be very helpful, thanks."

"Anything in the mail today?"

"Not a thing."

"So you haven't heard anything more about that possible domestic abuse situation?"

Em shook her head. "I haven't, and I've been on edge about it since the paper came out yesterday." She waved toward the stairs. "Be right back."

As soon as she opened the bedroom door, Byron shot out and

down the stairs. She chuckled, remembering how, only a short time ago, she'd had to carry him down those steps.

"Hang on there, pal. We need a leash first." She followed him down, grabbing the leash and harness off a hook in the hall. The dog wiggled impatiently. "Hold still, Byron. Let me get this on you."

When the door of the *Journal* opened and closed, Harley's friendly voice rang out. "Good afternoon. Welcome to the offices of the *Aspen Creek Journal*. How may I help you?"

"I'm looking for Emily Taylor."

Em gasped and did a double take, recognizing the voice. It couldn't be.

"Do you have an appointment?" Harley asked.

Em held Byron's leash and stepped into the reception area where her father stood. Her father. Dread and hope warred within her as they often did when he showed up. It was never a question of *if* he would let her down, but always when.

Still handsome and bigger than life, his hair held more silver than she recalled and there seemed to be a pallor to his face. Too much work and not enough golfing? A niggle of concern had her frowning.

"It's okay, Harley. This is my father."

"Your father."

"Dad, this is Harley Augustine. Harley, meet my father, Douglas Baker."

Harley's eyes widened, and her jaw slackened in stunned silence. "Nice to meet you, sir. I watch your legal segments on TV every evening."

Her father offered an amused smile at Harley's reaction. "Nice to meet you as well, young lady. And I'm delighted to have a fan."

"Oh, I'm certain you have many."

Em shook her head. If she only knew. Douglas Baker lived for his adoring fan base.

"Let's go into my office, Dad. It's right here." She led him into the conference room along with Byron.

Her father looked at the Labernese. "You know you have a dog there, correct?"

"Yes. I am aware."

Em frowned and worked to calm herself. Of course he would show up unannounced. The element of surprise provided leverage. He'd pulled this trick several times in the past.

"Have a seat. Give me a moment, Dad," she said on a weary sigh.

Em led Byron out of the room and turned to Harley. "I need a favor. Could you escort Byron to the dog park for me? Sarah is waiting to visit with him, and I hate disappointing her."

"Aw, I love Sarah. I'm happy to help," Harley said. "But we're going to talk later, right? Maybe I could take a selfie with your father. What do you think?"

"We'll talk later," Em said firmly. She walked into the conference room, shut the door and faced her father.

"You can't just show up like this without warning."

"If you had returned my calls I wouldn't have to 'just show up,' as you put it." He narrowed his gaze, scrutinizing her appearance.

Em didn't even flinch. After thirty-two years, her father's assessments and remarks on what he found lacking no longer fazed her.

"You look good," he said.

She blinked. "I do?"

"Yes. You seem happy. I'm glad."

"I am happy." She sat down and took a breath, unprepared for his approval.

"Apparently, you're doing a good job here as well. I overheard people in the diner talking about your newspaper."

"I am doing a good job." She paused to look him in the eye. "And I am not coming to work for you."

"I haven't asked you to."

Em would have laughed at that, reminding him of his track record of trying to manipulate her into the career he wanted for her, whatever that might be. Over the years his demands hadn't lessened. When she refused law school, he offered her the role of managing the social events for his vast entrepreneurial holdings. A glorified hostess. Then he suggested she come on board as the firm's public spokesperson. And on and on. Never once had he considered her hopes and dreams.

She stared at him for a moment. "Why are you here?"

"You're my daughter. Do I need a reason?"

She sighed. "There's always a reason."

"This time is different. I'm retiring."

Em frowned. "You've retired three times already."

"This time it's permanent. Doctor's orders. I have a cardiac condition, and if I want to live long enough to see my daughter get married, I have to slow down."

"Let's take the 'daughter getting married' stuff off the table. We've been there, done that, if you recall."

Em worked to stay calm. She and her father had a rocky relationship, but his mortality had never been part of the mix. This new information left her staggering. Despite his faults, he was her only living relative.

"What are your plans?"

"I've sold the house in Beverly Hills and left the firm. Bought a house in Denver."

"Denver?" She mulled his words. "What about those legal analysis segments on TV?"

He gestured with a dusting off of his hands. "Done with that as well."

"I'm going to need to speak to your cardiologist." She silently scrutinized his appearance. Impeccably dressed in dark slacks and a cashmere sweater, he carried a wool coat. Had he lost weight? She couldn't be sure. His face seemed puffy, and he didn't have his usual golden tan.

"You don't believe me?" he asked.

"Dad, you manipulated me into attending your alma mater, kept me in the dark about my grandmother's whereabouts and tried to buy me a fiancé. So, yes. I'm going to need the phone number of your cardiac specialist."

"Fine. And then what?"

"I..." She nearly sputtered. "You tell me."

"As I said, I've bought a house in Denver. I'll move in soon. I'd like to spend more time with you."

"You want to spend more time with me?" After all the years of ignoring her, failing to show up when she needed a parent, now he wanted to spend more time with her?

"Yes." His expression seemed sincere, if not uncomfortable as he looked at her. "I haven't been the father you needed me to be. For that, I apologize."

She bit back the sharp rebuke on her tongue. Could she trust him? The truth was, she desperately wanted to believe him.

"Okay, Dad," she finally said. "But this time we play by my rules."

"Whatever you say, Emily. I'm not here to negotiate. Whatever it takes to get you to agree to let me into your life, I'm willing to do."

Em nodded. "I'd like to have my father in my life. I'd like it a lot."

Five years and her father had changed. This was news fit for the front page of the *Journal*. Above the fold. She couldn't wait to tell Chase he'd been right.

Chase tapped on Harley's office doorframe.

She looked up and smiled. "Hi, Sheriff. I didn't even hear you come in. How's the campaign going?"

"The campaign? I don't know. You'll have to ask Cora-Lee."

His gaze went to the dozen red roses on her desk. "Nice flowers."

"Thank you. They're from Murph—I mean, Ryan." Harley's face pinkened at the words, her eyes sparkling. "Isn't he sweet?"

"He sure is." Chase had to smile. As he recalled, another letter in *Dispatches from the Heart* had dealt with how to show a woman you care. Murph must have taken notes. Good for him.

"Is Emily available?" he asked.

"Isn't her office open?"

"No, and I didn't want to disturb her."

"Oh, she had a visitor earlier. He must still be here."

The door to Emily's office swung open then, and a tall man with silver hair stepped out with Emily close behind.

Baker. Chase stiffened, immediately on alert. What was he doing in the office of the publisher of the *Aspen Creek Journal*?

She'd said she'd reach out to her sources. Was Douglas Baker her source? Was that why he was in town? The thought that she'd betray their friendship had his heart aching.

Emily followed Baker to the reception area. Then she spotted Chase and smiled. The kind of warm, welcoming smile he'd longed to see all day. It slammed into his chest, further confusing him.

Baker's gaze, however, skipped over Chase without recognition.

"Sheriff Everett. How nice to see you." Emily glanced from him to Baker. Despite the smile she'd shot him, she seemed tense.

He nodded curtly, noting that Baker's gaze immediately returned to give Chase a thorough assessment.

"Sheriff Everett, this is Douglas Baker. My father. Dad, this is Chase Everett, the head of law enforcement in Aspen Creek."

Father? Chase nearly stumbled at the information. He had no choice but to accept the hand Baker offered, though he provided no pleasantries in response to the man's brief greeting.

All these years, he'd wondered what he'd say if he were ever face-to-face with Baker again. Nothing could have prepared him for this moment. He didn't know what to say, because Baker had failed to recognize him. Then again, why should he? Chase hadn't changed the trajectory of Baker's life twenty years ago.

Chase wanted to be angry, but all he felt was weary. He'd spent a lifetime angry at the attorney who'd nearly put him behind bars. Now, all that remained was regret for wasting so much energy on the past.

Harley came out of her office and put on her coat. "I'm out of here, Emily." She smiled at Emily's father. "Nice to meet you, sir."

"Very nice to meet you, young lady."

"How did it go at the dog park?" Emily asked Harley.

"Just fine. Byron went upstairs when we got back. I assume he's sleeping it off."

"Thank you," Emily said. She turned to her father. "Dad, Sheriff Everett and I have an engagement this evening. Where are you staying? I'll call you tomorrow."

"Aspen Creek Inn." Baker reached out to offer Emily an awkward hug. He nodded to Chase.

When the door closed behind her father, Emily turned to Chase. "You're early."

"Why didn't you tell me that Douglas Baker is your father?"

She stared at him. "Why would I?"

"It's kind of a big deal that your father is a rich celebrity attorney."

"A big deal to who?" Annoyance laced her voice. "My father's notoriety has always been a burden to me. I'm judged by his yardstick, manipulated by his power and money. You can't imagine what it's like to have people think any success I achieve is because I'm a nepo baby. That's why I don't use his name."

"Why is he here, Emily? To get you a scoop about me for the *Journal*?"

She gasped. "Excuse me?"

He took a deep breath, pushing through the pain of the past to the pain of the moment. Had the woman he'd fallen in love with tossed him under the bus for a story? How had he not seen this coming?

"You think I'd exploit you to sell papers?" she said. Her face paled as she stared at him.

"Your father and I have a history, Emily."

Emily's jaw sagged. "What? I had no idea. What history?"

Suddenly, the sound of shattering glass imploding in the conference room reverberated.

Chase grabbed Emily around the waist and dragged her into the back hallway. "Stay here."

"What's going on?" Her face paled.

"The conference room. Those storefront windows."

"What? Why?" Her gaze met his, her dark eyes wide with fear.

"I don't know." But it didn't sound good, and he needed to keep Emily safe.

"Where are you going?"

"Stay there," he commanded. Chase inched to the front door and locked it. Crouched down, he assessed the damage in the conference room. Shards of glass were everywhere. A brick rested on the conference table at the spot where Emily worked each day and way too often at night. He shuddered at the sight.

Returning to the hall, he pulled out his phone and nodded to Emily. "Go ahead up to your apartment and lock the door. Keep Byron up there."

"What are you going to do?"

"I'm going to get a deputy over here to keep an eye on the place, and then I'm going to find Ennis Towers and arrest him."

"I don't understand. How do you know who did this? You didn't see who it was."

"Trust me, I know who it was, Emily. And I know it was the *Journal* that set him off."

"What does this have to do with the column?"

"You offered advice and she followed it. She left him. He blames you."

"Surely you don't think this is my fault. I had no idea who wrote that letter. And if the man who did this was angry enough to retaliate against the *Journal*, then maybe the *Journal* saved his wife's life."

"I didn't say it was your fault. You're right. You probably did save her life. But you could have been killed."

She frowned, her cheeks red. "Then why are you angry at me?"

Why was he angry? He was angry because he hadn't protected her. He should have worked harder to track Ennis down.

Chase released a breath. And he couldn't deny that he was angry because he'd trusted her with his heart, and she'd traded it in for a byline. She still hadn't explained why her father was here.

"We can talk later," he said. "Stay upstairs, please."

"Fine. But, please be careful, Chase."

"I will." From now on he'd be a lot more careful.

He punched in the number for dispatch and walked out the door.

Chapter Twelve

Em paced back and forth for an hour. The more she thought about what had happened, the angrier she became. She opened the bedroom window and looked outside. A police cruiser and a pickup truck she didn't recognize were parked in front of the *Journal* office, their lights casting shadows in the dusk.

When hammering started, she locked a whining Byron in her bedroom and went downstairs.

Ryan Murphy was in her conference room wearing overalls and putting up plywood where the window had been. He turned when she entered the room.

"Hey, Emily. I've got this covered. Literally."

"You swept up the glass?"

"Yeah. Although you ought to go over the room with a vacuum tomorrow. I'd keep Byron out of here for now."

"This is very nice of you. Send me a bill tomorrow, for the plywood and your labor."

"Nah. The labor is free for my friends. And, you know, thanks to you, Harley and I are…well, you know."

"I didn't do anything."

Ryan laughed. "Someday you're going to have to fess up."

"Not today," she replied, hiding a smile. "How about some coffee?"

"I'm good. Almost done here, then I'm meeting Harley for a

late supper. She'll want an update on what happened here. Are you okay with me sharing that information?"

"Of course. I was supposed to text her back and I forgot." Em glanced at the clock. She was supposed to have dinner with Chase tonight as well.

He hammered another corner and stepped back to evaluate the plywood. "That should do it. I've ordered the replacement window. It'll be here in about a week."

"Thanks again, Ryan."

"Not a problem. You know, I've lived here all my life. I can't recall something like this ever occurring. I'm real sorry this happened. Especially to someone who's been so good for our town. I hope Chase catches the guy."

"That means a lot."

He picked up his tools and tucked them in a large toolbox. "There's a deputy parked outside. He's there for the night. Chase's orders. If I were you, I wouldn't plan on crossing the sheriff. I've known Chase a long time, and I've never seen him so upset."

"That's my fault."

"Fault? You mean because he's in love with you?"

"What? No, he's not. He's mad at me. Furious."

"No. You've got it all wrong. Chase was scared you were almost collateral damage. He blames himself." Ryan shrugged. "I can't explain. It's a primal guy thing. We gotta protect those we love."

Em didn't know what to say to that. She couldn't even process Ryan's explanation. Chase Everett was furious. Plain and simple. She should have told him who her father was long ago, except she didn't want to be treated like Douglas Baker's daughter.

The puzzle was how Chase knew her father.

"You call me if I can do anything else. Oh, and lock the door behind me."

"I will. Thank you."

She shut the door to the conference room and stood in the reception area. What had happened tonight? How had everything gone so wrong? Grace's words echoed in her mind. *Will this decision unite Aspen Creek or tear it apart?*

Had she been carelessly playing with people's lives by creating the advice column? Could she have done something to help the man who threatened her? Perhaps it was time to retire *Dispatches from the Heart.*

She'd messed up. "Oh, Lord, how did I get it all so wrong?"

Chase banged on the door of the *Journal* the following day. *Lord, please let her answer before I lose the courage I need this morning.*

Finally, Emily appeared with Byron at her side.

She stared at him from behind the glass, looking as miserable as he felt. Finally, the lock clicked and she opened the door.

Chase stepped into the lobby. When he did, Byron knocked his head into Chase's knees. He gave the pup a good rub.

"What's wrong?" she asked.

"Nothing. I said we'd talk later."

"I thought you'd be by last night."

"I spent last night hunting down Ennis Towers."

"Did you find him?" she asked.

"Yes. He's in jail. Ennis admitted that he threw the brick."

She nodded slowly. "I'm sorry to hear that. I feel responsible. My job is to bring the community together. I've failed."

"That's not true. I don't think I made that clear—I was too upset last night. None of this is your fault—none of it. You've created something with the paper. Something that has folks laughing and talking." He met her gaze. "And this week, you saved someone's life. I'm in law enforcement to do what you did. You did it with written words. I'm proud of you, Emily."

"I'm very confused. This is going to take more coffee." She turned. "Do you want some?"

"No, thanks. I've been up all night drinking coffee."

Minutes later, she returned to the reception area with a mug and sat down in one of the chairs set out for the open house. Chase sat down across from her.

"We have to talk, Emily." Chase rubbed a hand over his face. He'd never been this tired in his life.

"It's almost 7:00 a.m. Harley's going to be here soon."

"She won't be here. I gave her the day off. I also took the liberty of canceling your breakfast meeting with your father. I told him you'd call back later."

"You what?" Annoyance flashed in her eyes. "Why would you do that?"

"I told you. We have to talk. Maybe you could start by telling me why your father is here."

"Apparently you were right." Emily took a deep breath. "It's been five years, and he's changed. I've been given a second chance to have a father in my life."

Chase didn't know what to say to that. Emily's words confirmed what her father told him this morning. Douglas Baker's arrival had nothing to do with him. While he was glad that she'd reunited with her father, he didn't know where that left him. Emily Taylor was the daughter of the man who'd nearly destroyed his life.

"And now you can tell me about your history with my father," Emily replied. "What happened that could have you even considering that I'd betray you."

Once again, he ran his hand over his face as shame threatened. It was now or never, if he hoped to, at the very least, make the woman he loved understand. The last time he was this scared was his day in court.

"Twenty years ago, my mother was the woman who wrote that letter to the *Journal*," he began. "My stepfather hit her.

And when he raised his arm to strike her again, I shoved him. Shoved him hard." Chase closed his eyes and swallowed, nausea overwhelming him. "That shove killed him." He looked at Emily. "I killed a man, Emily."

Emily stared at him, her mouth wide in shock.

"Your father was the attorney who tried to convict me of involuntary manslaughter. He pushed hard for the maximum penalty."

A soft anguished groan slipped from her lips. "I'm so sorry."

"It's not your fault." Chase longed to reach out and hold her but couldn't bridge the gap that still stood between them.

"Your family has been through much too much." She raised her head and met his gaze, dark eyes glassy with moisture. "My father didn't recognize you or your name yesterday. Did he?"

"I changed my name after I was acquitted. But, no, he didn't indicate that he knew me yesterday."

"You thought I was going to print that story. Trade our relationship to sell papers." She shook her head, her face crumpling. "How could you think so little of me when I care so much for you? I could never do that to you. To Hope or to Sarah. I've come to love them as well."

Her words punched him in the gut. She was right. He hadn't trusted their friendship. Their growing relationship.

"I apologize. The truth is, I've been terrified since you started researching for information on the candidates. Afraid for Sarah and for my mother. Last night I couldn't see straight. I was angry and scared."

He glanced at her and then away, shame haunting him again. "I couldn't find a single reason why you'd want to believe in a man with a past."

"Chase, we've all got a past. We all fall short. I care for you because of the man you are. You're that man because of your past. Your past has shaped you into someone with the compassion required to do your job so well. That's why you're going to be reelected. Everyone can see it but you." She took a deep breath.

"We have to tell my father who you are. He deserves the opportunity to make things right."

"I told him this morning. I went to his room at the inn, and we talked for a long time. Drank a lot of coffee."

Chase lowered his head and sighed. It was the longest two hours of his life since the long-ago trial. Facing his accuser and reopening those wounds and knowing he might have lost Emily, forever.

"You and my father? What did he say?" Her eyes widened.

"He told me he did recognize me and he was stunned. Then he apologized." Chase rewound that surreal moment in his head—Emily's father asking him for forgiveness.

She swiped at her eyes "I don't know how you can even look at me after what my father did. I'm so sorry."

His heart ached at her words. "Your father apologized for being so ambitious that he lost sight of his humanity and tried to prosecute a seventeen-year-old kid for a crime he knew that he wasn't guilty of." Chase released a breath. "He told me that he went home and sobbed when I was acquitted. Grateful for the verdict."

"Oh, Chase." Emily sniffed as moisture slid down her cheeks.

This morning in Douglas Baker's room, Chase had broken down. Emily's father had put his arms around him and asked for his forgiveness. Then they'd both cried.

Someday, he'd tell Emily.

Not today. He wasn't strong enough to tell that part today.

"What now, Chase?" she asked.

"Your father had a suggestion."

"Oh, no." She frowned. "I'm afraid to hear what it is."

"First, he told me I needed to forgive myself. And I guess he's right. Twenty years is a long time to hang on to something I could have turned over to the Lord long ago." He ran a hand over his face.

"You said, 'first.' Then what?"

Chase sighed. The hard part was coming. "He suggested I tell you that I love you."

Emily jerked back at the words. "You love me?"

"Yeah. Funny how that happens. You spend your life sitting in a boat fishing and happy to be alone. Then you meet a woman who turns your life upside down, and the fish and boat don't matter unless she's with you."

Emily sniffed.

"Do I even have a prayer of a chance, Em?"

"Chase, I've been in love with you for twelve years. So, yes. I think you have a chance."

Chase laughed with relief, his heart nearly bursting. He moved to the chair next to her and gently slipped his arms around her. Lowering his head, Chase kissed her.

"Ah, Emily," he whispered against her lips. "I don't know what I've done to deserve your love, but if you figure it out, let me know so I never stop."

Emily smiled and pulled him in for another kiss. "Chase, I have one question for you."

"Only one?"

"For now." She took his hand. "Are you the honest man? The one who wrote the letters to the *Journal*?"

Chase grinned. "What do you think?"

"I knew it was you." She leaned forward and kissed him again. "I guess we can put the column to bed now. It's served its purpose."

"Will you marry me if I ask or do you want me to write a letter?"

She laughed. "I'd love it in writing, but I don't want to wait on the post office."

"Emily Taylor, I love you. Will you marry me?"

"Yes, I absolutely will."

Epilogue

A week after the election...

"Today's the big day, huh, Emily?" Moss observed.

He stood in the foyer of Chase's house, now her house, too, with a cup of hot chocolate in his hand. Today, her favorite postal worker wore old-fashioned buckled galoshes with his wool postal jacket and pants. The ear flaps on his hat were snapped beneath his chin to keep out the biting wind, and a thick plaid scarf had been wrapped around his neck.

"Yes. We're headed to the county courthouse to officially adopt Sarah."

"That's wonderful. You deserve this," he said. "All of it."

"Oh, Moss. Thank you."

"Thanks for the cocoa. Warmed me right up." He handed her the mug and glanced around the living room. "Nice place you newlyweds have. The colors are soothing."

"That's what I told Chase the first time I saw his house."

Moss offered a mock salute as he opened the door. "Later, boss. I'll be praying for your little family today."

Em stood at the front door and waved as he strode down the recently shoveled driveway. Then she turned and headed into the kitchen. "Mail's here," she called.

"Anything good?" Chase asked. He moved behind her and eyed the stack in her hand over her shoulder.

"Postcard from your mother." She held up the cheery cardstock.

Chase took it from her fingers. "'Having a blast. See you soon. Love, Mom.'" He smiled. "I'm sorry she won't be here today, but glad she's following her dream."

"Like us," Em said.

"Yes," he agreed. "Like us."

She turned, put her arms around Chase's neck, and admired her engagement ring and wedding band. Getting married two weeks after Chase proposed had been an excellent decision. They'd both agreed that their love had been twelve years in the making. So why wait?

"When do we leave?" Em ran her fingers through the hair at his nape.

"How about an hour? I know it's early, but no telling what the roads are like."

"Fine by me," she said.

Chase smiled and leaned close to touch his lips to hers. "Would you fix my tie?" he murmured.

"Sure." Em quickly adjusted the material and patted it when she'd finished. "Very handsome."

"Do I look like a parent?"

"Absolutely. The parent to a seven-year-old girl and a one-year-old Labernese."

He chuckled. "Did the *Journal* come?"

"It did." She unfolded the paper and offered it to him. "Look at us on the front page, above the fold."

"'Sheriff wins election and takes a bride.'" Chase groaned. "Who came up with that?"

"Actually, it was Moss. He's expanding his feature writing. Sure, it's schmaltzy, but schmaltz will sell papers." She paused. "Oh, and did you know that Moss is dating Sloane Flanagan?"

"What brought those two together?"

"The love of bergamot."

He chuckled. "I heard a rumor that Murphy proposed to Harley."

"Yes!" She couldn't keep the excitement from her voice. "Yesterday. Harley is over the moon. How did you find out already?"

"Cora-Lee. I took the truck for gas last night and ran into her at the Gas and Go." He kissed her forehead. "Your column brought several happily-ever-afters."

"Oh, they would have figured it out eventually. Harley says it will be a Christmas wedding. Next year."

Chase took her hands. "Are you sorry we didn't have a big wedding?"

"No, though it took some time to convince my father that a wedding and reception at Cora-Lee's was what I wanted. Can you imagine what a circus it would have been if I'd given in? Television cameras and all his colleagues and celebrity pals." Em shuddered. "My new relationship with my father is based on boundaries. Lots of them."

She smiled at her husband, overwhelmed with love. "Our wedding was perfect. My father, your mother, Sarah, Byron and our friends. I have only sweet memories. No regrets."

"I'm glad."

Byron raced into the living room and out again.

"Can Byron come with us?" Sarah asked as she joined them. Wearing a sweet navy dress, with her hair in braids, she looked lovely and so much like her uncle.

The dog ran back into the room and sat at Sarah's feet, adoration in his eyes.

"I have good news," Em said. "Grandpa Douglas pulled a few strings. The judge is going to finalize your adoption in her private chambers, and Byron is invited."

"Oh, I'm so happy."

"Me, too," Em said. "Why don't you let Byron out to do his thing before we leave?"

"Okay," Sarah said. She skipped from the room.

Chase looked at Em and grinned. "Next to my wife, that's the prettiest sight I'll ever see."

Em smiled, fighting tears. Sarah had come so far.

"Is your father coming?" he asked.

"Yes, he's coming up from Denver. He'll meet us there." She looked at him. "What are you thinking?"

"I'm thinking that I am blessed beyond measure."

"We both are," Em said.

"I love you, Emily."

"I love you, too, Chase. Forever."

* * * * *

If you enjoyed Emily and Chase's story,
be sure to check out more books in
Tina Radcliffe's brand-new heartwarming series,
Aspen Creek Cowboys!
Available only from Love Inspired.

And discover more books by this author at
LoveInspired.com.

Dear Reader,

Welcome to Aspen Creek, Colorado. What a thrill to be back in the Centennial State, where I was blessed to live for eighteen years.

I hope you enjoyed Chase and Emily's story. Theirs is a story of not only second chances but trust. Trust isn't easy when we've been disappointed. Disappointment makes us think we can only depend on ourselves. The truth is that there is so much more waiting for us when we trust the Lord. He won't let us down, no matter the circumstances.

I've convinced the Soul Sisters to share some of their most popular buffet recipes. You'll find them on my webpage at www.tinaradcliffe.com.

I love to hear from my readers. You can email me at contact@tinaradcliffe.com.

Stay tuned for more stories from the Aspen Creek Cowboys series.

Sincerely,
Tina Radcliffe